BROKEN CIRCLE OF LIFE
By TL Bliss

TABLE OF CONTENTS

DEDICATION

Dedicated to the most important person in my life, my husband, my best friend. I thank God every day for bringing me this wonderful man.

Chapter One

Grace Elizabeth sat on the front porch of her home in Pennsylvania drinking sweet tea, and waiting for her daughter Lynnie to call. They were going camping at Pymatuning Lake in Linesville for the first time together. In fact, they were meeting for the first time as adults.

Almost twenty-five years had come and gone without the two of them having any form of contact. A child growing up without her mother to raise her, wipe her tears, fix her scraped knees, dress her up in adorable outfits, watch her first steps, make sure she had enough to eat, share her school memories, hug her, and all the other important things a mother does.

It did not seem real to be meeting the child she had had taken away from her so many years ago. What would she say? What would she do? Would Lynnie understand? Would this be a mistake? Should she just cancel the camping trip and see what happens?

The decisions were overwhelming her again. This surely was not the first time these exact thoughts had crossed her mind;

they had been tucked away in the part of her memory that was reserved for her daughter, Lynnie, only.

Deciding to leave well enough alone, she sat a bit longer and thought about all the years that Lynnie would be asking about; the history of what kept them apart for so long. She knew she would have questions for Lynnie too. They would equally share in the arena of wanting to know more about one another.

Grace Elizabeth also wondered if she would be able to keep her composure during the harder parts of answering the biggest question of *"why"* for Lynnie. She remembered it like it happened yesterday. Tipping her head back, she closed her eyes to see the pictures in her mind replay the past yet again.

After finishing dinner for the evening, everyone sat at the table drinking coffee and relishing in the day's affairs. The kids were outside playing in the pool and the adults were sitting around the outdoors table watching them throw each other into the pool and splash around having fun. Inside the house, I was helping clean up the kitchen after dinner was over. Ron was in the kitchen washing the dishes. Ron was the cousin of Rick and Rick was Lynnie's father. Connie was also inside having a quick cigarette break away from the kids before going outside to be with them. Connie was Rick's only sister. All of a sudden, Rick came running through the house chasing one of the younger girls in through the kitchen and back out the front door. Rick was bound and determined to catch her and throw her in the pool.

I peeked around the corner when the front door did not open after the two had made it through the living room running with wet clothes over top of the carpeting. I had seen Rick grab the young girl and spin her around, push her against the wall, and kiss her very tenderly and passionately on her lips and then he let her go to run away. I never said a word and went back to helping in the kitchen. This was not the first time I had seen this sort of thing take place with Rick. He was quite free with his want and desire to be with younger girls and usually tried to hide this only from his family members.

At first when I met Rick, he was a sweet, charming, handsome, blue-eyed guy who was eager to make you the center of his world and attention. You were all that mattered to him from that moment on. Until he managed to have his way with you and then it was the opposite.

Rick was very immature for his age and never wanted to settle down with any one girl alone, but did not show this side of himself to you until he had you caught in his devilishly handsome web. When Rick knew he had you wrapped around his little finger and could not stand it any longer that is when he knew he had you entangled in his cunning charm. It was not long after that Rick let everyone know the type of person he truly was.

While being played the fool and having had a baby with Rick, I only wished I had known about him and that he was that way prior to getting pregnant with Lynnie. Lynnie was an innocent, precious, and sweet baby who looked so much like her father Rick. As it turned out, I was just another statistic of Rick and his ways and sadly just another hash mark on his bedpost; like all the other women he had had children with.

When I went back into the kitchen, Ron was waiting for me there. Ron had seen the same thing I had seen in the living room and wondered how I was going to react. I shrugged my shoulders as if to say, "here we go again" and went back to drying the dishes. Ron sensed the sadness I had in my heart and offered me a friendly shoulder to cry on. I took him up on his offer and cried quietly for what seemed like forever.

Connie saw all of this taking place as if she was invisible to both of us, a fixture at the table decorating the space she was sitting in. Being Rick's only sister and family, Connie did not want to believe what she was seeing and soon there was a rumor of Ron and me having an affair.

The phone rang and it startled Grace Elizabeth. She was excited and was almost hesitant to answer, but decided it would be best to just show her compassionate side and be the mother she was never given the chance to be. She and Lynnie had this is common after all; neither knowing the other one and the opportunity to change this was quickly approaching reality.

Grace Elizabeth and Lynnie were finally able to arrange the camping trip that would reunite them after being apart for so many years. In a few short hours, the daughter she had given birth to would finally be face-to-face with her. Holding back the tears she felt welling up in her eyes, she decided to distract herself by going to check on everything she had packed to take on her trip.

Grace Elizabeth's motorhome was jammed full of photos of Rick, Connie, herself, and her family and friends to share with Lynnie. There were pictures of vacations she had been on to Myrtle Beach, the Outer Banks, Orlando, Arlington, Charleston, and other sites up and down the east coast. She and her husband, Lee, loved to travel and explore different areas and see as much as they could.

There were pictures of people that she wanted Lynnie to meet that Lynnie actually had known as a small child. There were pictures of people Lynnie had never had the opportunity to meet like Terry; the child of her grandmother Lisa and father Rick when they had their affair, Lynnie's brother who died tragically as a small boy, and Tammy who was Lynnie's best friend when they were very young girls. Tammy had been molested by Rick and she ultimately committed suicide when she could no longer bear the pain.

Hoping Lynnie would be willing to share these memories with her gave Grace Elizabeth all the support she needed to make this reunion happen. What questions would she have for Lynnie? Would Lynnie want to share her stories? Being reluctant to get all worked up about meeting Lynnie, she sat on the couch in the motorhome and recollected more about her own past.

Rick and I had just signed the papers to buy our new home out in the country. We were so excited and pleased to be able to have a place to call our own. It took every penny we had to come up with the down payment and this was not so pleasing to those who thought we needed to stay residing with them.

Lisa was my mother and a very deranged and manipulative person. She felt that she had to have control of everything in my life whether I liked it or not. Lisa considered me her "burden child" and never had any loving, nurturing, or motherly feelings for me in the least.

My sister Karen was her favorite child and Lisa made sure everyone knew that including me; to the point where Lisa had made my life a living hell. Karen was the best thing in the world to Lisa, as far as she was concerned, and Lisa never cared one bit for me.

I was the child Lisa always told me she "should have aborted" and I was "never going to amount to anything, nothing whatsoever." I was "bad luck" to Lisa and everyone around me, so Lisa felt compelled to be outright nasty and extremely cruel-hearted when I was around or involved in her life in anyway.

When Lisa heard of Rick and me buying a home, she was very dissatisfied to think that we would be moving out of her home. Lisa would no longer be getting the rent money we were paying her every month or the money she expected towards the utilities and groceries. More importantly, Lisa would not have any control over my life or me.

Lisa showed this anger by taking us to court for custody over our unborn child. Lisa was determined to see that our baby was not given anything that she deemed "unnecessary for the child to have"; Lisa did not want my child to have a normal life uncontrolled by her. Lisa would see to it that I would never have my baby with me or the chance to be a mother. She was determined to ruin my life in any way that she could

8

Lisa wanted custody so she could continue controlling me while enjoying every minute of my pain and misery. This was her game and she was going to win it. Lisa even went so far as to contact the bank where Rick and I had our new home loan and told them I was a drug addict and falsified my paperwork, and without stable employment, Lisa was not going to be responsible for the money I would owe for the home that I could not pay for.

Lisa was a very negative person who was raised by a very loving mother and a father who was not even her biological father; although, he took Lisa into his life as if she were his own. Lisa did not appreciate all that she had been given throughout her life and always wanted more from everyone.

My father Mel was a saint for marrying my mother and taking my sister and I under his wing; just like my grandfather had done with Lisa. Karen and I did not have the same father. My dad was Mel and her dad was some guy by the name of Tom; a drunk who was a fling of every woman in the little town they grew up in. There was not one girl Tom did not have in his bed at one time or another that lived in that town.

My father Mel was a very hard worker and had more love in his heart than any amount of men combined. My father was my guardian angel all of my life and my confidant. My best friend.

The phone rang again and this time it was not Lynnie. It was Lee, Grace Elizabeth's husband. Lee was checking to see what her plans were for the day so he could determine what he would spend his day doing.

They chatted for a bit and Lee asked, "How are you holding up? Are you getting anxious about meeting Lynnie?"

Grace Elizabeth replied, "Yes, but I am nervous." Lee could tell by the tone of her voice that she was an emotional wreck and needed his support, but neither wanted to overwhelm Lynnie with too much too quickly.

Lee agreed to stay home and wait for her to call to let him know when he would be able to meet with Lynnie. He was as nervous and anxious as she was, but he tried not to show it; although, she could tell.

Grace Elizabeth could not help but think of Lisa; how she was able to do all of the hateful and mean things she had been doing all those years. *Lisa always got her way, no matter what.* She knew that Lisa was a socialite in the little town they had lived in and played as many parts in the community in every way possible. Lisa wanted the world to think she was a goddess and a sweet, innocent, giving, gentle, passionate person. Little did the town know Lisa was not the princess they had all labeled her as being.

It was not long after the death of Tammy, Lynnie's young friend that the town caught onto Lisa's wicked and conniving ways. The people who lived in town that respected Lisa and sided with her were appalled at the different things that they themselves had helped her accomplish; even to the point of covering up Tammy's suicide.

The town banished Lisa. The friends and people she had known never helped her with another thing after Terry's death. Terry died at the young age of eight from a self-inflicted gunshot wound to the head. He had been playing with a loaded gun at Lisa's house when it fired cutting short his young life. The people in town never figured out what the real story was behind Terry or

Tammy's death basically because there was not enough evidence to charge Lisa or Rick.

There were people who "*surmised*" and people who "*knew*" what happened, but still there was not enough hard evidence to charge Lisa or Rick. Neither Lisa nor Rick was charged with anything, but they were both responsible for everything.

Lisa was able to get her way with the courts and police by manipulating stories to make everyone believe *she* was the damsel in distress, especially when it came to needing their help and support. Lisa was the one they were cheating on their spouses with and Lisa was the one willing to cover up stories and hide information for the shady cops in town, even the "do-gooders" that had something to hide.

In return, Lisa was given whatever she wanted, no holds barred. She traded her cruelty and was able to cover her devilish ways with sexual favors. Grace Elizabeth recalled being a little girl and waking up in the morning to see a different man's face lying beside Lisa. These faces were not the faces of men she knew and certainly was not the face of her father. She could recall seeing these faces when they had to go to court too, but nowhere else.

Grace Elizabeth's father was rarely home during the week and often he was gone for four to six weeks at a time. He was an over-the-road long haul truck driver and Lisa used that to her advantage. She knew where Mel was at any given moment of the day and was on friendly terms with his dispatcher and often times would just call to chitchat and could find out most anything she wanted to know about him. Her devilish ways always seemed to work to her advantage.

Grace Elizabeth realized she needed to focus on getting the final touches made for her trip to meet Lynnie. She still had some packing to do and preparations to get ready before the drive to Pymatuning Lake.

Grace Elizabeth was so nervous that her hands were shaking. Needing to regain her composure, she sat on the seat for a moment to calm down. Without even realizing it, she was recalling more and more to tell Lynnie.

During the brief time Rick and I had our new place, we managed to grow farther and farther apart. Finances were rough to say the least, with almost no money coming in at all. Rick was not working and stayed home with Lynnie during the day.

I was working at a local factory running a hot glue-banding machine and even though it was during the second shift, it was a good, steady job and had health benefits for all of us. Work had been slowing down over the summer, and some days we were sent home when the work just was not there for us.

One day, shortly after getting to work, it had been a slow barely productive day and with little to no work to do, the machine operators had been sent home early. While I was driving home, I could not help but wonder what Rick and Lynnie were up to, and how they would react to me coming home to spend the day with them; such a surprise after a long week and being gone so much trying to make some extra money.

As I drove into the driveway, I could tell something was not right, there were no lights on, and Lynnie was not playing outside. I immediately thought the worse and was in a panic. I stopped the car and jumped out, running towards the house. When I ran through the front door, there was Lynnie playing in her room with a safety gate up to her door so she could not

*come out and get into anything. Thank
goodness, she was safe!*

*Where was Rick I wondered? He
was naked and in bed with the young girl we
had used as a babysitter on rare occasion. I
was furious! I was fiercely angry and was
having trouble controlling my rage. Rick
started laughing as if it was some sort of
joke and this just made me even more upset.
Nancy, the naked babysitter was scared and
trying to gather her clothes in a big hurry,
as she stumbled over the bed sheets draping
onto the floor.*

*I waited for Nancy to leave the
bedroom and followed her out to the living
room to the front door that I held open for
her, pointing my sharply extended finger in
the direction she needed to be moving in. I
also voiced my regard making sure she knew
that she would no longer be babysitting for
us ever again.*

*Slamming the front door, I returned
to the bedroom where Rick was still lying
naked on top of the barely made bed. He
looked like a hunter that just shot the biggest
beast of his life, all brave and full of himself.
I decided that this was the time for him to
feel the pain that I had been feeling for so
many years; I wanted him to hurt and I*

wanted him to be afraid. I wanted him to know this was not a little girl that he was still playing games with, and I wanted him to know that I had had enough.

I drew back my tightly clenched fist and let him have it square on the jaw, gripping onto my own fingers as hard as I could I swung with every ounce of strength I had! Furiously, I struck him, swinging for all I was worth, repeatedly, until he begged me to stop hitting him.

With his face all covered in blood and his jaw a bloody mess, I stopped swinging and just stared at him, glaring into his eyes. I wanted him to see the anger and the rage I had for him. I wanted him to see what I had been seeing; all the years he had been so abusive towards me. I wanted his eyes to meet mine. The baby blue eyes I had loved waking up next to every morning, the eyes I could see my future in, the eyes I saw my daughter in; his baby blue eyes that were covered with red swollen skin and blood seeping out and running down onto his cheek.

My heart had so much pain that I cried for days. Lynnie and I stayed with my grandmother for a few weeks until I could gather myself up and face my harsh reality.

We were going to make it and we were going to be just fine. I was determined not to be the person Lisa always said I would be, and I knew I did not want to be anything like Lisa, not in the least. I was stronger than Lisa was; I was stronger than Rick was; I was the woman I wanted to be and was not ashamed of who I was any longer.

I did have the courage and ability to overcome the abuse and heartache. I knew in my heart that I had to have the strength to continue on and be the person God had wanted me to be. I was going to make it, no matter what!

Realizing that she had gained enough self-control, Grace Elizabeth started the motorhome up and began down the road headed for Pymatuning Lake.

Chapter Two

The traffic on the way to Pymatuning Lake was horrible, even on the back roads that no one ever traveled. There was more traffic out that day than Grace Elizabeth had ever seen and she figured that Lynnie would have a rough time traveling as well. She even figured Lynnie might be later than they had both anticipated.

Driving into the park, she made sure her reservations were all verified, and thanked the Park Ranger for her help.

Grace Elizabeth drove the motorhome through the tent section watching the families already there, seeing the kids running and playing, watching the dogs chasing the kids, and the parents setting up tents. Everyone was enjoying the sunshine and making memories as a family. She caught a glimpse of a woman that would have been Lynnie's age and wondered if it may be her, but it was hard to tell from behind, so she kept meandering slowly through the campground until she found her site and parked the motorhome there.

She could not help but wonder if she was going to be emotionally able to handle reuniting with Lynnie without Lee there.

Lee was Grace Elizabeth's best friend and God sure knew what He was doing when He joined their two worlds together. All of Grace Elizabeth's strength came from God and Lee; they both had always been there for her, even if only in her heart. She knew they would help her through this.

Grace Elizabeth saw the Park Ranger driving through the campground. The Ranger had stopped to talk with one of the families who were camping nearby. While the Park Ranger was visiting with the camper parked right beside Grace Elizabeth, her emergency radio blared with a voice reporting a motor vehicle accident that happened on the highway not too far from the campground. The woman's shrill but stern voice on the radio also stated that the coroner had been called to respond to the accident.

A few moments later, a man's voice came over the Park Ranger's emergency radio and stated that a young couple had been killed in the accident. Grace Elizabeth could not help but let her emotions get the best of her and she immediately started crying. The tears welled up instantly, and all she could think of was Lynnie. Grace

Elizabeth hoped and prayed Lynnie would be safe.

Grace Elizabeth dropped to her knees with her hands folded in prayer and asked God to help her make it through this. Grace Elizabeth asked Him to give her the strength to persevere and prayed that the families of the victims would seek His help and comfort in their time of grief. She had to take a moment before getting back up; this news had shaken her quite badly and she took her time getting back to her feet.

Grace Elizabeth tried to call the phone number that Lynnie had given her in case of emergency, but no one answered. She was growing more and more concerned for Lynnie's and her safety, praying that Lynnie had not been a part of the accident.

Just then, a little car pulled up out front of the motorhome. Grace Elizabeth did not recognize the vehicle and instantly feared the worse. She reluctantly stepped outside to see who it was and what this person wanted. The lady stepped climbed out of her car.

"Did you hear about the accident?"

"Yes, I heard it over the Park Ranger's radio a few moments ago."

Grace Elizabeth was looking at the lady with tears welling up yet again in her eyes.

"Can I ask you what your name is?"

"I am Patty, the lady who owns the bookstore down town."

A sudden rush of relief came over Grace Elizabeth and she never really heard what Patty had to share with her, other than the words she uttered about the young couple being two kids who were driving drunk and wrecked their car; local kids.

As she thanked God repeatedly in her own mind for sparing Lynnie from harm, Grace Elizabeth went inside to unpack and get ready for her meeting with her daughter.

Grace Elizabeth had unpacked the groceries and put them away in the cupboards. Then unpacked the towels and wash clothes she had folded freshly and placed in the laundry basket. She also had to go outside and plug into the electrical box, hook up the water connection and sewer line so she could have all the amenities of home.

Once everything was unpacked and everything was neatly in its place, Grace Elizabeth decided to make a pot of coffee. Sitting there on the couch waiting patiently for Lynnie to arrive, she could not help but reflect back in time yet again remembering more of her past.

After breaking Rick's jaw in several places and leaving him for good, I was convinced that Lynnie and I could make a life for ourselves and be free from his vicious torment for the last time. We had rented a small apartment down town that was simple yet perfect, and just what we needed.

Lisa was furious that I was not under her roof where she could control Lynnie and me. She called my dad and told him that I had the baby in the apartment with no food for her to eat or diapers for her to wear. She also spoke with Rick conniving and scheming different ways that the two of them could take Lynnie from me.

She would see to it that I would not have my daughter with me and that was all there was to it. According to her, I was the most unfit mother alive. I could not help but chuckle at the thought of Lisa, of all people, saying that I was the most unfit, but who was I to pass judgment. I was more fit to be a mother than she ever was. I at least wanted the best for my daughter and wanted no harm to come to her, unlike Lisa.

Lisa was furious to think that I would have anything good in my life after "ruining hers". Lisa had taken Lynnie and hid her from me. She was bounced from Lisa's friends, to total strangers, to friends of friends just to keep us apart. The police in our town helped Lisa manage to keep Lynnie from me. She had her tools of her arsenal all prepared to use against anyone who dared to stand in her way too, which meant that she got whatever she wanted. She even dared to tell the police that I had been beating Lynnie. Just remembering the past made me furious. Oh, the audacity of that nasty woman!

Even the memories were getting to be too much to bear. With the officers, neighbors, and other town members Lisa's friends, I never stood a chance defending myself against these horrible people because Lisa had them convinced that I was a terrible person and that I was not able to take care of Lynnie. Lisa also told these "friends" of hers that she herself would make sure Lynnie was safe and away from me. Her friends helped her hide Lynnie from me too.

It was too late for the men in town to do anything to protect Lynnie and me when they realized that Lisa had been lying all this time. She had used these people to help hurt me and they had kept everything a secret so their wives and girlfriends would never know the truth behind the affairs that had been taking place. Each man had their own story and each man had their own piece of the pie. Little did they realize that they too were breaking the law; they realized this a little too late to do anything to help.

Another time during my life where I asked God for His help, and prayed that He would see me through; I prayed for the strength and courage to protect Lynnie and myself no matter what Lisa was up to.

I had retained a lawyer to help protect us from the wrath of Lisa and Rick. Since Lynnie had Rick's last name, it was rather difficult for me to keep her from him. I never wanted to separate the two; after all, Rick was her father. The attorney told me that I could take Lynnie from Lisa since I *was the natural mother of the child, so this was my goal – to set up a meeting at Lisa's house and take Lynnie back; using everything within my power, even physically if need be.*

Dad could not make it to the meeting, as he drove tractor-trailer over the road and was not even on the east coast, but my grandmother said she would surely be there. I went with whatever support I had available and set up the plan to have us all there together.

When I arrived, Lynnie came running to me with arms wide open. I dropped down to my knees and scooped her up hugging her and smothering her face with kisses. Just then I realized Lisa was pouring coffee and grandma was letting the dogs back in, both were distracted; so I darted for the door with Lynnie in my arms. Lisa dropped the coffee pot, ran over to where we were, and grabbed me around the throat with her arm in an attempt to stop me.

I screamed for her to let me go and she would not release the grip she had on me; she pulled her arm tighter and tighter until I just could not breathe anymore. Grandma came and took Lynnie from me; I was still holding onto her tightly, and that was all I remembered before I passed out. When I woke up, the police were there and I was lying outside on the grass where Lisa had obviously dragged me. She told the police I was trying to break in and she was forced to defend herself, which was a total lie, but because it was technically Lisa's property, they were not willing to listen to my side of the story and she demanded that I be removed from her property.

When I told the police that I was not going to leave without my daughter Lynnie, Lisa stated Lynnie was not there and never had been. She told the police they could come inside and look if they wanted. She had Lynnie removed from the house while I was passed out. I never did know where she had gone or even who took her. I knew this was going to be an awful fight, especially when my own mother was willing to choke the life out of me while I was trying to protect my daughter.

The police did their due diligence and removed me from Lisa's property. She chuckled as the police helped me up from the ground. She knew she was getting away with almost killing me and there was nothing I could do about it, any of it, not even to defend my own daughter or myself.

The smell of the freshly brewed coffee made Grace Elizabeth realize it was getting closer and closer to the time when Lynnie should be arriving. She had decided to make herself look a bit more presentable, combing through her hair, and washed her face off with a cool washcloth. It was a gorgeous bright sunny day; the weather was perfect for being at the campground. The birds were all chirping, the kids running around playing with each other, and nature was providing a beautiful background for a picture-perfect reunion outside. The lake was calm and the sunlight glistened off the water with a marvelous reflection.

Watching as the neighborly campers with their families were spending quality time together made Grace Elizabeth realize exactly what she had been missing with Lynnie. She had missed Lynnie's first steps, first day of school, doctor's appointments, school pictures, drawings that Lynnie made, holidays, her first bicycle ride, her first new dress, her first boyfriend, basically the majority of her first *everything*.

Grace Elizabeth knew she had missed the most important part of Lynnie's life growing up and felt compelled to find a way to make this up to her daughter. She knew that neither Lisa nor Rick could stand in the way of their reunion and she wanted this to be a special occasion; a day for her and Lynnie to remember. The meeting of a lifetime for both of them, literally was about to unfold for each of them.

Grace Elizabeth was getting ready to bake some cookies when the phone rang again. It was Lee calling to check on her.

"Lee, did you hear about the horrible accident near here? It seems a couple of young teens were killed in a car crash not too far from here. The book store owner Patty had stopped in the campground to say hello and she told me the young couple were local kids from here in Linesville."

"The news on the radio has been reporting heavy traffic and said to be careful while traveling. The police departments are advising no unnecessary travel due to the high amount of traffic on the roadways already."

"Good thing I am here at the lake already and all set up. How do I get the oven to work so I can bake some cookies?"

Lee was the cook in the family and Grace Elizabeth never had a reason to light the oven. Lee talked Grace Elizabeth through the procedure with step-by-step instructions.

While the two were talking on the phone and the oven was warming up, a car pulled beside the motorhome.

"A fancy, little red sports car just pulled up outside, I have to go; it may be Lynnie. I love you and will call you later."

Grace Elizabeth hung up the phone, glanced out the window again, wiped her sweaty palms off on the towel attached to the handle on the oven door, and stepped outside to see who it was.

There was a young woman who climbed out of the fancy little red sports car. She had long brown, curly hair, just like Grace Elizabeth. She knew in her heart that it was Lynnie and looked up to the Heavens and thanked God for answering her biggest prayer. Lynnie, her daughter, was standing there with her, finally.

She could see a mix of emotions on Lynnie's face and in her eyes. Lynnie was almost hesitant to keep eye contact. Speaking quietly she said, "Lynnie?", as the tears welled up in her eyes, a big smile came over Lynnie's face. The tears spilled over running down their faces and they both started crying.

Lynnie ran to Grace Elizabeth and hugged her the same way she had hugged her so many years prior, just like the day of the meeting at Lisa's home when the attempt was made to get Lynnie back. This time there was no one there to separate the two of them. No one there to come between them. No one there to prevent the reunion from happening. No one to come between mother and daughter. The reunion they both had waited for was finally taking place.

Grace Elizabeth said quietly to herself, "Thank you God for this day and this chance."

She just could not stop crying, happy elated tears kept strolling down her face knowing that He was the one who brought the two of them back together again. All of the anguish that was building up and felt for so long was released as they stood there and holding onto one another, not wanting to let go.

They decided that it was time to gather their emotions. They were together now and there was no looking back or stopping them this time. It was safe to stop hugging Lynnie because there was no one there to take her away. No one there to do anything to prevent them from being face to face. No one there but the two of them together. They were finally safe from *all* harm.

Once Lynnie's belongings were out of her car and put away in the motorhome, she moved her car over to the parking lot at the end of the road. She walked back to the motorhome and was ready for a cup of fresh coffee. As they sat there for a moment, Lynnie kept looking at Grace Elizabeth like there was something missing.

She would look deep into Grace Elizabeth's eyes for a brief moment, but then pull her glance away and look down; as if she could not believe they were there together and she was silently confirming that it really was Grace Elizabeth.

There was so much to catch up on and they were both very eager to start asking each other the questions they really wanted answers to. Grace Elizabeth suggested Lynnie get a chance to relax after driving so long, make herself comfortable, and get a nice hot shower, and then the two could sit and talk. Lynnie agreed and gathered her shirt and shorts, grabbed a towel, and proceeded to get into the shower. Listening to the sound of the shower running made her glad that Lynnie was finally there with her and she drifted into thought again.

I knew this was going to be a long road for Lynnie and me. Lisa would see to it that I would not have anything good in my life and tried to turn my father against me as well. He was not ever going to let her come between us. Karen had asked for a loan to buy a car that she really wanted and asked dad for the money. When dad said that he did not have the extra to give to her, Lisa gasped and shrugged her shoulders while asking dad if he had been giving his money to me again. He replied with "no" and she very sternly voiced her dislike of how he had been helping me out every now and then. She wanted no more of this and she made it very clear that she did not like his actions in the least.

I was struggling with life, emotionally, and financially, and dad was doing what he could to help me. I worked at the factory still, but the money that came in was not always enough to last until the rent was due again. Lisa told dad that he had better never give me any money for anything, no matter what. If she heard of him giving me anything, she would divorce him and leave him broke and begging in the street. I could remember hearing her say these words to him on several occasions at different times during my life. Her words tore through my heart knowing that my dad was only trying to help me out and she was not in the least bit going to allow this. Dad also knew that she would never leave her main source of income broke and begging in the street because then she would have to go to work and that was not about to happen. He was safe even though her sharp words stung like salt in an open wound.

This never kept my dad from helping me and he was always glad to help however he could, and even more so after Lisa's threats. My dad even bought me the next two vehicles I had and Lisa was never the wiser that the money had come from dad.

Just then, the shower shut off and a few moments later Lynnie was walking back out drying her hair with a towel.

After sitting together for a while, they had decided it was time to find out more about each other. Lynnie grabbed some cookies and another cup of coffee and they both headed for the couch.

33

Lynnie was excited to be there with Grace Elizabeth, but Grace Elizabeth could tell there was obviously something wrong and was hoping to eventually find out. After seeing Lynnie look at her eyes and back down again, she asked Lynnie what was weighing so heavy on her mind.

"I am just so happy to be here with you, finally."

She had waited a very long time to get the chance to meet Grace Elizabeth, her mother. She had heard stories about Grace Elizabeth, but often wondered how true they were. She also heard quite a few lies from her Grandmother Lisa and was a little reluctant to share those with Grace Elizabeth.

She started with the first question and asked Grace Elizabeth, "What happened all those years ago to separate the two of us?"

Grace Elizabeth reflected back again on the time she found Rick at home with the babysitter, but was not sure that information needed to be shared in that much detail with Lynnie. Lynnie had always been fond of her father and Grandmother Lisa, and Grace

Elizabeth did not want to sway her opinion either way.

Grace Elizabeth knew Lynnie would be able to find it in her heart to come to her own conclusions, but did not want it to be the person who destroyed Lynnie's bond with the only family she had ever known.

"I want you to be honest with me, no matter how much you think it will affect me. I am a big girl now and can make my own mind up, but I want to hear the truth; the *real* truth. I deserve to know why you and I had been kept apart for so many years."

"I appreciate your candor Lynnie. I will be perfectly honest with you and tell you whatever I know. The *real* truth, as you call it."

"Thank you. I really appreciate your honesty."

"When you were just a young girl, your father and I had some difficult times that we were facing. He wasn't able to find work and we had just purchased our new home. He was distraught at not being able to provide for us. Or so I thought anyway."

She could feel herself getting a little nervous; her hands were starting to sweat just a little.

"Your grandmother offered to let us stay with her until we could get back on our feet again. So, we decided that letting the house go back might be the only chance we had at catching up financially. So, we went to stay with her. When we realized that things just were not going to work out, with the conflicts from all of the various personalities under the same roof, we decided that maybe your father needed to go back home with his family and see if he could find work out there. After he was gone for a while, actually he was gone for a very long time; I knew that he wasn't ever going to come back for us."

Lynnie sat there listening contently while shaking her head back and forth in awe of what she was hearing.

"In the meantime, your Grandmother decided that she wanted me out of her house. She felt it was time for me to be on my own and told me that I could not take you with me. Her reason behind you staying there was that since you had your father's last name she would keep you there with her until I was financially able to have you with me. I did not realize what her intentions were at the time."

Grace Elizabeth could feel the tears that had spilled over her welled up eyes and roll down her face.

"Your grandma forced me to leave and she hid you from me Lynnie, so I could not take you with me. One time, she even had the law physically remove me from her property. I tried to get you back and hired a lawyer to help us, but that did not work either. The lawyer was more of a waste of my time and money more than anything."

Lynnie watched the facial expressions that Grace Elizabeth portrayed as she was talking and knew that she was telling the truth when the tears rolled down her cheeks. All she could think was how horrible this must have been for her mother to endure and how wrong that these feelings had all been retained inside for so many years. It was literally heartbreaking to see her cry like this as she was talking.

"Your grandma also helped your father hide you from me and they told the authorities that I had abandoned you. Which in turn, by my so-called abandonment, the courts gave your father full custody. I never knew the story they were telling the courts until the attorney I had hired found this out when we managed to find you one time. The contact she had at the courthouse said that it would be useless for me to even try to get custody since I had abandoned my rights as your biological mother and gave all of my custodial rights to your birth father, which hearing this infuriated me. The attorney and I were both shocked and astounded."

Wringing her hands a little bit and adjusting her position a bit, Grace Elizabeth continued on.

"My attorney left the decision up to me as to whether I wanted to pursue any further. She said it would be very expensive to try to fight them. I had no money and both your grandma and father knew they could win since I was so impoverished myself. Every time I would find you, your father moved further away with you. This went on for years and years. Your Grandma Lisa hung your pictures in her house to show that she knew where you were and gloated over the fact that she knew how miserable I was. I swear she even chuckled at the tears I was shedding every time I looked at your photos."

Lynnie stopped Grace Elizabeth at this point.

"I was told a completely different story."

"If you don't mind Lynnie, I would like you to tell me what you were told."

"I will tell you everything I know, but it probably won't make much sense since it was all lies."

"Grandma Lisa told me that you ran away with dad's cousin Ron after a pool party at Aunt Connie's. Dad said you were living with Ron and left me with grandma so the courts would not put me in a foster home."

After a brief hesitation, Lynnie continued on.

"Grandma Lisa also told me that you were doing drugs so heavy that you couldn't afford your rent or food, so she was forced to take me away from you. I was also told that you left me with strangers and grandma couldn't stand the thought of me being thrown around at just anyone and said that I would be better off if you had been…dead."

The words stung Grace Elizabeth's ears. She recalled being told roughly the same thing by Lisa so many years ago so she knew there was some truth to what Lynnie was saying.

"Grandma also said that I did not need you in my life to bring me down. I would be better off without you. Grandma even suggested that maybe she needed to get custody of me so she could be sure that no one would do bad things to me ever again and dad almost gave her custody of me."

Lynnie stopped talking for a brief moment. She sat back and hung her head down.

"Wow this is harder than I thought."

"I never heard of you trying to provide for me; I was told that the only reason you gave me to grandma was so you did not have to find a babysitter when you wanted to go to the bar. Dad told me the same story, so I always assumed it was the truth. I didn't realize they were both lying about you and always had been. I wish I had been strong enough to know what they were up to. I could have saved myself a lot of emotional torment had I only listened to my heart."

Grace Elizabeth was crushed to hear what they had been telling Lynnie. The words tore through her like a knife. She was consumed by overwhelming bitterness towards Lisa and Rick for these horrible nasty lies, but tried not to show it. How could she expect anything different from the two people who were so determined to make her life a living hell?

She assured Lynnie this was not the case and apologized to her for having to hear the *real* truth after all these years. Grace Elizabeth knew telling her the truth would change her feelings towards her father or grandmother, but she wanted her to know the truth. After all, Lynnie deserved to know the *real* truth, not the continued lies from people who cared less how she really felt.

Grace Elizabeth knew it was not right to judge Lisa and Rick for their mischievous lies and knew they would eventually get what they too deserved. They would have to answer for all of the lies they had been telling for so long, and all of the hurt they caused. Their judgment day was between them and their maker.

Grace Elizabeth found it difficult, but contained her thoughts.

"I tried for many years to find you, and every time I managed to get close your dad moved you farther away. I sent you packages in the mail when you were little. I used to talk to your stepmother, Deb, every now and then just to see how you were. Deb told me that she would tell you stories about me and show you pictures. She told me that she would tell you about your birth mother and share what she could with you. Your dad caught her showing you pictures of me and made her leave the house. He threw her out in the street with nowhere to go and no one to help her."

"I recall momma Deb telling me that times were sometimes difficult for her and dad, but I never knew this before now."

"All of her family was in the northern states and you were all in the south. Deb told me that your father made her throw out the packages I sent down there to you. She also told me she would read you the cards and give you the money from them, but never told you where it came from so your dad would never know. She also told me that she would give you some of the gifts I had sent to you and retape the boxes before throwing them out, but again did not tell you where they came from so your dad would

was supposed too, as long as I went when I was supposed to. We had made this agreement when he originally had gotten sick quite a few years ago. There was one point where we thought he had lung cancer, but thank goodness, he didn't; all the tests came back negative."

Lynnie let out a breath in relief.

"He had a lung collapse while he was driving over the road and the doctors made him come in for more tests. Your grandfather was quite the stubborn man when he wanted to be. He did not like anyone interfering with his life and he felt doctors interfered too much. He had his own medical home remedies. He preferred to grab another bottle of NyQuil and fix things himself."

Grace Elizabeth felt her mind wandering with the thought of her father.

"Well, now I am just rambling on; I better get back to my original statement. The Sunday in question that I had talked with him, I was checking on him over the phone, and I could tell quite a bit about him by the sound of his voice. I did agree to leave him alone, but told him I would call back later to check on him again. He agreed. I waited a few hours and called again. He sounded even worse, so I told him I was coming over to take him to the doctor whether he wanted to go or not. To my surprise, he actually agreed! I was so shocked that he agreed to go that I grabbed a few things, threw them in a suitcase, and headed for his apartment, which was about three hours away."

This was the hard part for Grace Elizabeth to put into words.

"When I arrived at Grandpa Mel's, his door was locked and I had been in such a hurry to get there that I had forgotten his house key. I never even figured that I would need it since he knew I was on my way. I knocked on the door and there was no answer, no sound inside, nothing. My heart skipped a few beats and it felt like my stomach was tied all in knots when he didn't answer my knock. I knew something was wrong. Fearing the worse, I called the maintenance man to have him come and unlock your grandfather's door so I could get inside."

She hesitated for a moment. After taking a deep breath, she was able to continue on.

"When the door was finally unlocked and we could get in, Grandpa Mel was lying face down on the floor in a puddle of his own blood. He had fallen off the commode and landed face-first on the cement floor. He died before I had a chance to get to him."

Grace Elizabeth hesitated long enough to wipe her eyes and grab another Kleenex to blow her nose.

"I have harbored these memories for so long, knowing that I should have gone sooner, but he asked me not to come up. I did not expect to see him lying there dead on the floor when I arrived. I will always be ashamed of myself for not going sooner to check on him. I blame myself for not being there to help him when I needed to be. I could have saved his life had I been there. He died alone, lying there face down, on the floor."

Lynnie hugged Grace Elizabeth and consoled her as they both cried together. This was such an emotional time that they were sharing. Grace Elizabeth did not think she had that many tears left after professing to be such a strong person all of her life. She was always the one who held everything together and now she needed to be held together.

They just sat there in the silence drinking coffee and not saying a word for what seemed to be quite a while, almost as if they were giving him a moment of silence in remembrance.

Chapter Three

Grace Elizabeth wanted to hear what her daughter's life had been like after they had spent so many years apart. Lynnie decided it was time she share a few things about her life.

It was her turn to tell Grace Elizabeth the truth and said, "I knew you were out there somewhere, but I had no idea where. I could hear dad and Grandma Lisa talking about you, but I never knew if it was really *you* until they mentioned your name. I was able to put together in my mind the information I overheard, with the cards and gifts that momma Deb shared with me. I always assumed that you and I would meet up again one day. I would know it was you from the pictures I saw; the pictures Deb showed me and would say to me, "*This is your mother and her name is Grace Elizabeth. She loves you very much and misses you Lynnie. She asked me to give you a hug every night before tucking you in to sleep*" and you would be this same woman from the pictures. I said my prayers every night and asked God to bring us together again one day."

Grace Elizabeth put her forefinger to her lips hushing Lynnie.

"My dear sweet girl. Do you believe in God?"

"Yes ma'am, I sure do. I had to have someone to believe in since my life was so full of the unknown and for a little kid that can get really scary. I used to pray that God would help me find you. I knew He would answer my prayers and bring us together one day. God was always there when I had no one else who would listen and He was there to help me make it through the tougher times. I would love it if we could pray together; you and me?"

Lynnie went first and said with her head bowed in prayer holding onto her mother's hands.

"Dear God, thank you for bringing Grace Elizabeth and I together today. Thank you for watching over her and keeping her safe from harm. Thank you for joining our worlds together once more, finally. Thank you for reuniting us today and mostly for being present in my life as my strength, Savior and for my guidance. Amen."

Grace Elizabeth went next with her head bowed in prayer, tears rolling down her cheek, and holding on tightly to Lynnie's hands.

"Dear Lord, thank you for answering all of my prayers and bringing my daughter back to me. I had faith in you to do so on your own time; when you felt it was right. I know things have not been easy for Lynnie and I thank you for watching over her when I was not able to. Thank you for the help of Deb who shared the knowledge of me with Lynnie. Most of all, thank you for helping us see each other again. I say this with a meager heart and pray for your forgiveness. Amen."

They sat there silently for the next few moments cherishing the moment and savoring what they knew in their prayers to be a true act of being reunited at the will of their savior. Without Him, they would still be lost souls on the journey of finding each other, lost in their tormented wilderness, souls on the hunt for some peace.

After a bit of time had passed, Grace Elizabeth was curious about how Lynnie was able to find her.

"So Lynnie, how did you find me?"

"I was searching online for you using the information I had gathered over the years. I knew we looked alike in some ways and I also knew your name. I knew you were in Pennsylvania since Grandma Lisa said that was the last place she knew you were. I eventually just put the pieces to the puzzle together and then one day I found some contact information. I tried calling the number, but it had been disconnected so I kept looking."

Grace Elizabeth knew that her daughter was smart, but didn't realize how smart until now.

"I managed to find another address and phone number for you. I put the address in my GPS and drove until it said I was at my destination. I did not want to call and be heartbroken again over another disconnected phone number and figured the address was not far, so I may as well drive. I was at your home a few months ago. I remember seeing this same motorhome sitting in the driveway, so I know for sure it was your address now."

The motorhome was what she remembered after all this time. She thought that was clever.

"I was never able to get any information out of my dad or Grandma Lisa, other than their hatred mixed words for where they wished you were rather than where you truly were, so I had to find you the best way I knew how. I knew you were out there looking for me too and we would eventually find each other."

Grace Elizabeth was fascinated by Lynnie's ability to research enough places to be able to find her, narrowing her location down enough that she actually had found her. Knowing herself how tedious, dull, and uneventful trying to find someone could be; knowing the process generally leads to brick walls and forks in the road for most people. Lynnie had made finding a needle in a haystack seem easy.

After they spent the majority of their time reliving the past and bringing up the memories that had been put to rest over the years, they had both decided it was time to talk about more recent events occurring in their lives.

"Where are you living? Where do you work? Any boyfriends? What are your hobbies?"

"I am living in South Carolina, near Charleston, in a town called Summerville. I have been there for the past few years now and I love it; sure feels like I belong there, very homey to me. I work for myself, mostly photography and writing books. Even though Summerville feels like home to me, I have very few friends there and in Charleston."

Grace Elizabeth recalled her last trip to Charleston and it brought a somber feeling to her.

"I am not the type of person to hang out in bars; I do not drink or go to any of the clubs. I usually just stay by myself at home. I had been married for a little while, but that didn't work out. His name was Tim and he was gorgeous. He was my best friend, even if only for a short amount of time. He was having an affair and I never realized it until after I was pregnant with the twins."

Lynnie hesitated before continuing on with her statement; knowing she had to tell Grace Elizabeth and she dreaded bringing the memory back to life, even if for a brief moment to share with her mother. She gathered enough courage in her heart to continue telling her story.

"I was pregnant with twins and lost them shortly after I found out about Tim's affair. When I found out about his 'girlfriends', I confronted him, we argued, and with the stress…it caused me to have a miscarriage. The doctor told me the babies were both girls, but they weren't fully developed, not enough to live. The overwhelming time mixed with the stress devastated my body and the girls didn't survive. I barely survived losing them and could have really used some support from either you or dad."

Feeling her heart melt with Lynnie's words, Grace Elizabeth felt closer to her daughter more now than ever.

"Grandma Lisa did not believe me that I was even pregnant and dad just shrugged his shoulders as if he could have cared less. I had nobody, nobody at all to comfort me, no one to convince me that I needed to go on. I struggled with the memory and hurt day after day, and prayed for forgiveness for losing my babies because I lacked common sense. I should not have let it bother me as much as it did, I should have just walked away, but I could not go on knowing that he lied about *everything*."

Stopping to gain her composure, Lynnie took a deep breath before continuing on.

"He eventually married one of the girls he was cheating on me with, and married her rather than grieving his own children's death. He never truly grieved his loss. He was too busy with all of his 'girlfriends' to realize he had lost two girls; his *own* children, his baby girls. I held a small funeral service for them and they are buried in South Carolina. I guess that is the real reason why I am still there. I cannot force myself to leave and not take them with me. I will more than likely be there for the rest of my life. They are like glue holding me there."

Lynnie was really opening up with Grace Elizabeth. She wanted to give her the chance to keep whatever was in her heart and on her mind. More importantly, Grace Elizabeth was waiting to hear Lynnie call her "mom" and know that it really came from her daughter's mouth. She had waited to hear those words since Lynnie had been taken away, but wanted *her* to say it.

She cringed to herself and just did not feel right hearing Lynnie saying 'momma Deb', even though this is how Lynnie knew her and that was a part of her past; an area she felt she had no right to intervene.

"I started writing books about the different places I traveled to and taking pictures. I take a lot of pictures and brought my camera with me too. I want to capture as much of *us* as possible and I would really like to have someone take our picture here together. I did have a couple tabletop books with pictures published, pictures from the traveling I have done. The books are mostly landscape and wildlife, but it paid me some fairly decent money. I don't really have any other hobbies. About all I do is photography and traveling."

Feeling like now was the perfect time to mention Luke, Lynnie spilled the beans about her new fellow.

"Although, I have been dating a guy I met in Myrtle Beach when I was there earlier this year. Luke is his name, well Lucas really, but everyone calls him Luke. We have a lot of fun together. He does a lot of photography too and owns a shop in Charleston. He sells photography and pictures that show the real, genuine beauty of Charleston. He is a great guy and we have a lot in common. I enjoy spending time with him. He makes me laugh, which is a daunting task at best. I have a couple of my pictures on display in his shop."

Listening to Lynnie talk was like looking in a mirror. Lynnie had the same likes and dislikes as she did, and they shared some of the same hobbies. It was pretty evident that Lynnie was her daughter and she was really cherishing this time that they were sharing together. Just her and her daughter; as it used to be, a moment in time with just the two of them enjoying the company of the other. Memories were being made again, cherished memories with her beloved Lynnie.

It was now her turn to share some stories about some of the different events that had taken place while she and Lynnie were separated. Even though she was really enjoying Lynnie's life stories, she knew Lynnie was also eager to learn as much as she could about her birth mother, as the memories she did have were vague and few in number since she was such a small girl when they were torn apart.

"Well, it is pretty obvious that we share the same blood Lynnie. You and I both have the same hobbies. I love to travel and take a lot of pictures. I have boxes and boxes of pictures from the different places that I have been. We have been all over the east coast. I love Charleston and that entire area. Actually, Lee and I were looking at some property down there not very long ago.

We have decided that we want to be able to spend winters in the south and keep our place here in Pennsylvania for the warmer summer months. We haven't really decided where we want to buy land, but we do know it will be in South Carolina. Lee was born in Charleston."

Lynnie grinned hearing her mother say she and Lee were looking at buying property in South Carolina.

"Oh, wait until you meet Lee. He is truly my best friend. We have shared quite a lot him and I. I sure don't know what I'd ever do without him. We both enjoy spending our time together, traveling all over the country, and watching car races. He loves the car races and fishing. I just recently learned how to do a little fishing. I am not much of a fan yet, but I could see where it has its advantages. He is truly my best friend and I thank God every day for bringing the two of us together. We have been through some real trying times together and we always seem to weather the storm for one another and with one another."

Grace Elizabeth loved talking about Lee. He was her world and she wanted everyone to know just exactly how much she truly loved him.

"We share a storybook romance; love at first sight and romance as if it were right out of a book. I would like you to meet him. I'm sure you will find him to be quite the perfect gentleman."

"What do you do for work? I'm sure all of this traveling you do and this gorgeous motorhome wasn't free?"

"Well, Lynnie, I work mostly for myself and have for many years. I review medical records and make sure the information is accurate before the physician signs his name on them. It can be a rather difficult and monotonous job, but I love it just the same. I get to work from home, or wherever I have an internet connection, and it keeps me with traveling money. Lee takes care of everything else financially. He is the real 'moneymaker', not me."

Grace Elizabeth figured this would be a good time to tell Lynnie about Mike.

"Lynnie, I do have to tell you something that may upset you, but I feel you should know."

"Well, you have my interest piqued, what could you possibly have to tell me that would upset me after all these years apart? I could never blame you for anything, ever."

"Ok, I'm just going to throw it out there. Here it is; you have a brother. He is nineteen months younger than you are. His name is Michael and he lives with us here in Pennsylvania."

She could tell that Lynnie was a little shocked by this news and only hoped that it would not upset her very much. After all, she did warn her to be prepared for what she was about to say. Mike was waiting for her to call so he could drive to the lake and meet his sister. Lee would be bringing him tomorrow unless she called and asked that they not come just yet.

"I have told Mike about you and he is waiting patiently to meet you. He loves the thought of having an older sister, even though you both have never met. Mike and Lee are both waiting for me to let them know if they can come meet you tomorrow."

Lynnie was not upset, but in fact was actually overcome with joy to hear that she had a brother. This meant that she really did have a family out there and she appreciated and thanked God silently to herself for bringing her and Grace Elizabeth back together. *Her mother*, how those words rang music to her ears. She really wanted to meet both her *new stepfather*, Lee, and her *new brother*, Michael. She had a family, a real honest to goodness family.

They talked for so long neither realized that they had consumed two pots of coffee while sharing stories. They figured they had better eat something before they went on any further. They each made a sandwich made from leftover meatloaf and warmed up gravy that Grace Elizabeth brought from home.

While they were sitting there eating, they both realized the moment that had made them both so anxious had come and gone. They were in each other's company for the first time since Lynnie had been so viciously taken away from her.

It wasn't bad, it was the best feeling Lynnie had for quite some time. Learning about her family and enjoying every moment of her mother's company.

After a night sleeping in the chair and on the couch, they woke up confused as to their whereabouts. Then it dawned on them that they were at the campground and had fallen asleep talking to each other into the wee hours of the night and next morning. Hearing the birds chirping and kids waking up was a delightful sound. The outdoors life was waking up and the sounds of the day were soon waking everyone up.

They each gradually started to come around. They had grabbed a quick shower and made more coffee to help wake up. Today was a brand new day and Grace Elizabeth and Lynnie had a lot more catching up to do.

Grace Elizabeth was wondering if Lynnie would want to meet Lee and Mike today. She never really said yes or no either way when Grace Elizabeth mentioned it to her just yesterday. She was very excited, but never really said anything. They sat at the table sharing the new morning together and this was the perfect opportunity to see what the day held in store for them.

"I would like to have both Lee and Mike come meet you today if you are up for it. I also have some pictures and other family information that I want to share with you. I know that you may be a little overwhelmed with all of this, but I want to make sure you are comfortable with all of this newness in your life first. They will understand if it is just too much for you to take right away."

Remembering her own medical records, Grace Elizabeth also needed to let Lynnie know she brought a copy for her to keep.

"I remembered to bring some medical records with me so you would have some history to take with you, as far as hereditary issues and genetically speaking of course. Just let me know if this sounds good or if you have something different planned for today."

Lynnie sat there dazed and wondering, with a smile on her face. She had a sense of calm over her that she had never felt before; she was relaxed and her mind was not afraid to soak up her thoughts.

For the first time in her life, Lynnie had a family – a real family. She was so consumed with the concept racing around in her mind that she clearly forgot that she was pouring coffee and spilled it all over the countertop.

"Mom have you got any paper towels?"

All Grace Elizabeth heard was the phrase, *"Mom have you got any paper towels"*, and she was instantly overwhelmed with happiness. She had finally spoken the words Grace Elizabeth waited so long to hear; her daughter had called her *mom*.

Once Lynnie realized that she had just called Grace Elizabeth *"mom"* for the first time, she started crying. She found that she was overcome with joy to hear the words herself and imagined Grace Elizabeth was too. Everything was falling into place just as Lynnie had hoped it would. She had a mom, stepfather, and a brother all in the past 24 hours. How could a person go wrong with this sort of news?

Lynnie was sure she wanted to meet Lee and Mike now. This would be the icing on the cake in her world and she just could not resist the sweet temptation that life had offered up in front of her.

Chapter Four

Grace Elizabeth called Lee on his cell phone and told him that both he and Michael could come meet Lynnie. Lee was very excited to hear this and went to get Mike out of bed.

"Mike, you need to get up son. We are going to the lake to meet your sister today. Try not to take too long or take too much time getting dressed now. Wake up and grab your shower; I will get breakfast going and will meet you in the kitchen."

Mike was excited to be meeting Lynnie for the first time in his life. He heard childhood stories from his mother and was anxious to get to meet his sister. He jumped up out of bed and knelt down on his knees beside his bed to say a prayer before going to the shower. Mike placed his hands together, closed his eyes, bowed his head in prayer,

"Dear Lord, I want to thank you for bringing all of us together. I am excited to meet my sister Lynnie and I am more grateful that my mom has finally had some closure on her sadness and wondering. We are all very grateful and thank you! One more thing, thank you for making my mom so happy; she really deserves to have some good in her life after growing up with so much bad. Thank you! Amen."

Mike jumped back up to his feet and headed for the shower.

Grace Elizabeth was preparing for the guys to arrive and realized that her world was finally what she had envisioned it to be so many years ago. It was all starting to come together for her and there was no way she was going to let anyone tear it apart again.

If Grace Elizabeth had known when she was younger that standing up for her own rights was what she needed to do, then obviously none of this would have ever happened. She also realized that she needed to stop blaming herself so much for things she could not change. What had happened was in the past and she now had a future with her son *and* daughter. She felt blessed finally having the life and family she had longed for and never thought would ever come to be. She finally had everything she ever wanted, felt content, and was the happiest she had ever been.

While the ladies were waiting for Lee and Mike to get there, Lynnie took out some photos to share with Grace Elizabeth.

"This picture was taken when I was younger and Grandma Lisa thought I looked so cute with my curls all neat and shiny with my ponytails. I loved that pink dress; it was my favorite."

"This picture was taken when I graduated high school. I really enjoyed going to school and learning different things. I liked being away from home and not having so much stress and tension. It was my way out of the house and I took advantage of it every time I could. Looking back now, my friends were my social outlet and I needed their attention. I went to the community college for a few years for English and Computers, but couldn't afford to keep going so I dropped out before I earned my degree."

"This picture is my favorite and the only picture I have of you and me together. Deb gave it to me when I was little. Sorry, it looks like a puzzle taped back together but dad tried to tear it up and throw it away; he even lit it on fire once. Thank goodness, he fell asleep and only the corner was burned."

Grace Elizabeth had noticed when Lynnie mentioned Deb that she did not call her "momma Deb" as she had been. She wondered how this was going to affect the relationship that Lynnie and Deb shared. After all, Deb did raise Lynnie the majority of her younger years. Shrugging this thought off her shoulders, she went back to Lynnie and her pictures.

Lynnie continued on with a sad look on her face, but was not teary-eyed.

"This is a good picture of me when I was pregnant with the twins. I was huge and it seemed like sundresses were all I could find to fit me. This is still so hard for me to believe. I have what I call my "mommy spells" and cry myself to sleep holding onto this picture. I was such a mess when all of this happened and I lost the twins. I often wonder what they would look like now and what they would be like. Would they have brown curly hair like we do? Would they be little troublemakers ransacking the house? Would they have pudgy little cheeks that you could just squeeze? I sure wish things would have been different and the twins had lived."

Grace Elizabeth stopped her from talking and just hugged her; letting Lynnie sob on her shoulder.

Feeling Lynnie's sadness and being able to relate to the "loss" of a child was a similar bond that they shared. Although she had her child taken from her and spent all those years not knowing if Lynnie was alive or where she was, whether her daughter was safe, if she was eating or hungry; all the same things that Lynnie was feeling.

The remorse of losing a child, even in the separate instances, was unbearable to think about right now and she just wanted to hold onto her daughter and help ease her pain.

They went back to looking at more pictures. Grace Elizabeth was showing Lynnie some of the family she had never met before.

"This picture is Lee, your stepfather. He is a kind, gentle, very loving man; he is my gift from God. I know that He brought us together so I could have the strength that Lee provides for me. He is my guardian angel just like your grandfather once was. He protects me and takes excellent care of us. He is also one of the best cooks I have ever met."

Lynnie took the picture from her mother's hand to have a better look at it. Lee was a handsome man with slightly greying hair and the bluest eyes she had ever seen. Her dad's eyes were blue, but nothing like his eyes; they were amazing. She had a sense of calm looking into his eyes and felt comfortable knowing this was the man who had been taking care of her mother and brother.

Grace Elizabeth handed Lynnie another picture.

"This is a picture of your brother Michael. Mike, as we call him. He was born nineteen months after you and no one in the family ever knew about him. I didn't want to have him taken away from me too. I could not bear the thought of losing another child, so I moved away and no one ever knew I was pregnant."

Lynnie sat looking at the picture of her brother. How amazing to go from being all alone to having a brother too.

"I was almost afraid to tell Lee that I was pregnant for fear of him leaving me, but prayer and love brought me the strength to share the news with him and we were married before Mike was born. We were both so happy and this was a good time in my life, even though I was missing you and worried sick over the thought of you not being safe; out there all alone."

Lynnie looked at the picture of Mike with a smile on her face; this was her brother! He looked a lot like Lee, with brown hair, tiny curls, and he even had blue eyes too. Mike's eyes were as calming as Lee's and Lynnie loved that about the two of them. To Lynnie, the eyes were the window to a person's soul and she saw comfort and love looking into their eyes through the pictures. Lynnie was overwhelmed to think that her life was heading down the path of being complete. She was glad that she had so much love to welcome her into this new phase of her life.

"This picture was taken when Lee and I were married. We wanted a small private little wedding, so we contacted the mayor of our town and went to a peaceful little community park where we were surrounded by flowers and sunshine. The park was being cleaned that day by some young teens from the church's youth group.

They saw that we were getting married and asked if they could watch the service; of course, we did not mind at all. It had been sprinkling a little rain prior, but when the mayor was ready to begin, the rain stopped. The service went without a drop of rain until after we were pronounced man and wife, then it started to sprinkle again. The sun was out while we were having our little service and we knew it was God smiling down on us with acceptance."

Lynnie took the picture and held it for a long time just looking at Lee and Grace Elizabeth embraced in a kiss. She knew that was the storybook kind of love she was looking for and wanted.

"Is there a copy of this wedding picture that I could have?"

She wanted to be able to see the happiness that Lee and Grace Elizabeth shared every day. Grace Elizabeth handed Lynnie a box of pictures that she had prepared for her.

"There are copies of all these pictures in this box for you."

Grace Elizabeth handed Lynnie a big shoebox wrapped with light purple paper and had a ribbon on the top of it.

"Thank you!"

Lynnie realized there were no pictures of her Aunt Karen in there and wondered what ever happened to her and where she was. Lynnie had not been in touch with the family for so long that she did not know where any of them were, other than Rick; her father. He was in New York living with another girl who was pregnant with his baby. She had so many stepbrothers and sisters that she lost count after each of Rick's overnight flings left him. She realized that she might never have a close relationship with any of them since their mothers moved them all away and there was not enough time in her life to find them all.

Lynnie was glad that she come to Pennsylvania and had the opportunity to meet her mother and share in the stories of her life, even if some were hard for her to hear. She wanted the truth and knew that she was finally getting this after waiting so long to find solace in knowing what happened to separate them.

Chapter Five

Lee and Mike were headed for Pymatuning Lake to meet up with Grace Elizabeth and Lynnie. The weather was a gorgeous sunny morning and the two of them were filled with joy to be able to meet Lynnie.

Mike was excited that he had a sister and wanted to know everything about her. He wanted his sister to be an integral part of the close-knit family he grew up knowing.

Mike knew the meaning of a loving family. He grew up with Lee for a father and Grace Elizabeth for a mother; the best parents a kid could ask for. He treated them with respect and loved his mom and dad very much. He was content and knew he had the best life, but adding a sister to the mix would make it even more special for him. He grew up a child of God, even though it can sometimes be tough for a young man to believe in the Lord, especially when he felt that society leads the weak and sometimes destroys their finest intentions. He tried to share everything in his life with his parents and the Lord. Knowing that his life was a gift from God to his parents, he wanted to share this with the world. He wanted to let everyone know how he felt about his Savior and how much he appreciated being a Christian. To him, God was a member of the family; the best friend he had ever had; most importantly, *his* best friend.

Mike had a special person in his life and her name was Annie. She was a fair complected young lady who had blond hair and green eyes. She was a schoolteacher and loved children. They were planning to get married soon and he was eager to share this news with his sister.

Lee wondered how Grace Elizabeth was doing. He missed having her home with him last night, but knew she needed to be by herself when meeting Lynnie. He knew that she did not want anything or anyone interfering with their reunion. It was not an easy decision to have him stay behind, but he knew she had her reasons and he respected her for as much. He knew that his wife was prepared for the worst and possibly best outcome; either way she was ready for this meeting and would handle it just fine. He also knew that she was not alone and that God was there by her side, helping his loving bride to make the right choices, and calming her fears. He knew that if he trusted in the Lord and his wife, now was the time to prove it. His biggest fear was Lynnie rejecting Grace Elizabeth as her mother, but he knew deep in his heart the chance was slim for this, but also knew there was still that chance too.

Lee had the perfect life, a loving wife, and great son. He worked hard to provide for his family and he cherished every moment he could with them. He knew God had given him everything he asked for and answered his prayers and for this reason, he thanked God every day.

Lee thanked God for bringing him to Grace Elizabeth when he had and that she gave a second thought to pulling the trigger that would have ended her life. He thanked God for sparing the woman he truly loved. He thanked God for giving him the best friend a man could hope for and he woke up next to her every morning. Lee was convinced that he was the happiest man alive!

Lynnie and Grace Elizabeth were preparing brunch for the guys when they arrived; working together hand-in-hand to make sure everyone would have enough to eat, chuckling back and forth about the memories the two of them were making, and asking more questions about each other.

"Lynnie there are some things that you must know about me that I want to tell you before Mike and Lee get here. This will be very upsetting, for you to hear, but I want to be the one to tell you. Please sit here with me and let me share this with you."

Lynnie sat down beside Grace Elizabeth where she patted her hand.

"Lynnie, after you were taken from me and before I had met Lee, my self-esteem was destroyed, I felt hopeless, and I was at a very low point in my life. I was living in fear of what could possibly go wrong now that I was alone and I felt truly all alone; almost hollow I was so alone. I feared waking up every morning to solitude and not knowing what was going to happen next. I hated myself and was not a very nice person. I did not care about anyone or anything. I was distraught and knew in my heart that the devil was working hard to destroy me. The devil worked so hard on my self-esteem that I let myself go, on the inside and out. I was a mess to look at and I was an even bigger mess inside; I was broken into a million tiny bits. Despair was knocking at my door and I was ready to let it in."

"Mom, you're crying and it is making me cry too."

"I knew that I was never going to have a relationship with my mother where I would be loved by her or even *liked* by her; she just simply would not allow that to happen. Grandma Lisa wanted me out of her life forever and she was paying the devil to torment me. All I really had going for me was your grandfather Mel. He was my guardian angel my entire life, but he was gone all the time working and I did not see much of him after the family split up. We talked and shared a little time together, but not as often as either wanted. I was alone. I had no one but myself."

Grace Elizabeth grimaced a bit, adjusted herself in her seat, and continued.

"This is where it gets hard for me Lynnie, so please bear with me."

Grace Elizabeth wiped her tears, reached out and took ahold of Lynnie's hands.

"I had planned to take a trip to Charleston, South Carolina, and I was going by myself. I packed no clothes and only took one bag with me. This bag had contained a .357-magnum and a handful of bullets. I was prepared to end the misery and take my own life. I mentally could not and did not want to live anymore with all of this pain and hurt my heart had in it. I wanted to be free of the devil and Grandma Lisa for once in my life. I parked the car down by the battery wall in Charleston and watched the dolphins play in the water there. I loved looking at the Rainbow Row of painted houses and had secretly longed to live there one day."

Lynnie knew of the exact spot Grace Elizabeth was talking about. This was one of her favorite places to go.

"I knew that this was the safest place I could be to take my own life. This was the place I wanted to leave the world; no longer just *existing*. Here in what I considered to be all of God's beauty, I begged for His mercy, took the gun from the bag and made sure the barrel was loaded. I sat there looking at the gun in my hand, nodded my head knowing that this was the answer to all my problems. I cried thinking of you and missed you terribly, but knew I had no choice other than to be free from the pain and to end my despair. I sat there for quite a while crying and looking down at the gun in my hand. I knew now was the time and I closed my eyes and raised the gun to my head. My hands were shaking and the tears flowed like the water running from a waterfall. I could not believe that this was my only way out of a life that I did not want to live anymore. I managed to get my hands to stop shaking and was ready to pull the trigger, but Lee saved me."

"How did Lee save you?"

"He had been sitting in a car parked near me and had been watching me the whole time I had been sitting there. He was not sure what the object was I had in my hand at first, but he soon realized it was a gun and came to help me. I was shocked to think that he came to save *me*. I did not think I was fit for saving and I was thoroughly convinced of this. I told him to go and just leave me alone, threatened him with the gun, and he never left me. He managed to calm me down enough that he was able to unload the bullets and put the gun back in the bag."

"Now that truly is a miracle. What a marvelous thing for him to do."

"He held me for hours listening to me talk. He wanted nothing more than to make sure I was safe. We talked for hours sitting there watching the water. It gave me great comfort to know that someone was interested in how *I* felt and what was wrong with *my* heart. Lee never left my side after that day; we have been together since that day. He held on to me and thanked the Lord for making him go to the battery that day because he had no intention of leaving the house on his only day off, but something inside him told him that he needed to be there. I am sure it was God who sent Lee to the battery that day to save my life."

Lynnie sat there with her head hanging down just soaking in the words that she was hearing. The tears rolled down her cheeks and Lynnie did not care; her heart was breaking to think that Grace Elizabeth almost took her own life. To think that her mother had so much pain in her heart to end it all with a bullet; how much she despised her Grandma Lisa for making Grace Elizabeth feel this way. How could a mother make their own child feel so horrible about themselves? She spoke silently to herself asking God to forgive her for feeling so much hate towards her Grandmother Lisa. She never wanted to feel that much hate for anyone and kept asking God to forgive her.

Lynnie hugged Grace Elizabeth and cried on her shoulder for yet another time. She hugged her mother as tight as she could.

"Thank you for sharing that with me, I know it must have been hard for you."

Grace Elizabeth and Lynnie shared a special bond with each other after she told Lynnie about this moment of her life. Lynnie knew she loved her mother and wanted her to know that she did.

"Mom, I love you. Thank you."

Grace Elizabeth sat there with a look of happiness and contentment on her face.

"Thank you Lynnie, I love you too."

Knowing that Lynnie knew about Grace Elizabeth's past and being able to share it with her was all that mattered to Grace Elizabeth. She had heard the words from Grace Elizabeth herself and it strengthened their bond.

Chapter Six

Lee and Mike had just arrived at the front entrance to Pymatuning Lake. They were there to meet Lynnie and they were both very excited. On the way to the park, they talked about how they were going to be appreciative of having this day, no matter what the outcome was going to be. The guys each had questions for her and answers prepared for her questions as well. They had tried to put themselves in Lynnie's shoes and imagine what her life had been like, what she would look, and what she was like as a person.

The guys pulled up in front of the motorhome and Lynnie and Grace Elizabeth were sitting inside silently and still hugging each other after the story Grace Elizabeth had just shared with Lynnie. The ladies wanted to freshen up a bit and each washed their face with a cool washcloth and brushed their hair back, trying to be a little bit more presentable.

Lynnie opened the door and just could not contain herself. She headed right for Lee and just hugged him, crying into his shoulder, never uttering a single word. She knew this was the man she would be happy to call her father for the rest of her life, even though she had never met him before. She sobbed and hugged Lee tighter and tighter.

"Thank God for you. You are a true blessing to my mother. I cannot tell you how much I appreciate the love you have given her all of these years."

"Thank God for you and this reunion. I am proud to be a part of your mother's life, and now yours too Lynnie."

Lynnie walked over to hug Mike next and Mike grabbed Lynnie and held onto her tightly. He cried on her shoulder, thanking God that they were together. She could not control her tears either and both stood there hugging each other and crying together.

"I prayed to God that we would meet one day Lynnie; I prayed for you every day. Thank you and thank God for bringing us together."

"Thank you for being there for mom. I am proud to call you my brother Mike. Thank God we are all finally together."

Lee and Grace Elizabeth were standing beside Lynnie and Mike. They too were crying and whispering to each other.

"I am so grateful for this day. I am thankful that we have shared the opportunity to be together as a family after all of these years. My life, heart, and family is finally complete now. I have told Lynnie everything I could think of to tell her in the short amount of time we have been here together. She knows about Charleston, she knows about her father and Grandma Lisa. She knows."

Lee stood there silently watching his family bond together. He knew that this is what God had intended when He brought Grace Elizabeth and him together at the battery that day. He knew that one day all of his prayers would be answered, and he also knew it would be done in his Lord's time, not his. He knew that his purpose in life was to be the father that he did not have to be, the father that Lynnie never knew could possibly exist. He knew he would cherish this moment, this special moment in time, and he started sobbing and silently prayed to himself.

"Thank you Lord for bringing all of us together. I knew you would answer our prayers and we would all be together in Your presence one day. Thank you for bringing Lynnie home to us and for bringing us to her. Lynnie has many prayers that will need your guidance and we are all here to help her through this time in her life. We all need your support and love. We are all bonded by your mercy and love. Thank you Lord, thank you!"

Once all of the tears stopped flowing and everyone was able to put a smile back on their face, they all sat down at the table thankful for being a complete family now.

While they were all enjoying the silence and just soaking in the moment, Mike's cell phone rang. It was Annie. She had called to see how he was doing. Mike told Annie that they were all at the campground and he was meeting his sister Lynnie for the first time.

"Lynnie looks just like I thought she would, with long brown curly hair and she looks just like mom. She is really here Annie. I just can't believe it. My sister is here."

Annie was eager to meet Lynnie and asked when a good time to come to the lake would be. Mike was not sure how to respond, but stated that anytime would be good as far as he was concerned.

Lynnie was overwhelmed with all of the emotions she had experienced in the last twenty-four hours. She went from being a single child, living alone in the middle of Summerville, South Carolina, all by herself, to having a complete family; a mother, stepfather, and a brother. Lynnie had a brother that was very handsome with his curly brown hair and blue eyes. Lynnie had a stepfather who had the most gorgeous blue eyes in the world and loved her mother very much. Lynnie was finally part of a true family, *her* family.

The weather at the lake was not always sunny and beautiful. The blue sky had turned grey and cloudy, and the wind began to blow. The wall of rain was moving across the water rather quickly. The sky opened up and the rain began to pour down. Lee, Grace Elizabeth, Mike, and Lynnie all covered their heads with whatever they could get their hands on and headed for the motorhome to get out of the rain.

Lee had made another pot of coffee while everyone sat in the living room talking and getting to know one another a little more. Especially Mike and Lee who were eager to get to talk with Lynnie.

Lynnie knew that the guys would have questions, so she started out by giving them a brief overview of her life so far.

"I am so glad that I finally had the chance to meet you Mike and you too Lee, in person. I have a family now and that feels like heaven on earth to me. I have been living in Summerville, South Carolina, for the past few years. I work with photography and I write books; though I mostly do photography. I was married once for a short time. I was also pregnant once. I lost my twin girls due to stress I created to my body when I found out that my husband was having an affair and I confronted him. I have been alone since separating from Tim. I dated a few men since, but nothing very steady. I am currently dating a man named Luke. He owns a shop in Charleston where I have some of my pictures for sale. Luke is a nice guy and makes me laugh. We met when I was at Myrtle Beach earlier this year. I guess I am just too vulnerable right now to truly fall in love, but he has been good to me so far."

Feeling like she had covered most things up front, she decided to toss in a bit more.

"I do not communicate with Grandma Lisa or Rick, my biological father, and have not for quite a while. I started searching for my mother and they were both very offended by this. They practically disowned me when they found out. My Aunt Karen wouldn't even talk to me when she found out. I figured it was their loss and chalked it up to that. I wanted to find her and get the truth. She was the only one who would tell me the truth; after all, what did she have to lose after all these years."

Listening intently, the guys were drawn to her words.

"I knew in my heart that she was out there and I wanted to find her. I searched and searched. I even found an address online and drove to the location to see if it was mom's house and sure enough, I finally found her. I drove by her house a few times; even remember seeing this motorhome parked there. I never stopped for fear that someone other than mom would answer the door. I did not know what to say and knew if she answered, she would know who I was."

Lynnie got up from her seat and poured another round of coffee.

"I had a wonderful lady that I call Deb, well I did call her momma Deb until I met my real mother. Deb was a great person. She raised me with the truth about my mom and showed me pictures of her. She would read me the cards and gave me gifts that Rick told her to throw out. Deb had saved the cards and gifts to give to me, but never told me who they were from until I was older. She made sure that I knew who my biological mother was. I knew in my heart that God would answer my prayers and bring me to her and He did."

Grace Elizabeth sat there listening to Lynnie speak and could not help but wonder if there were more to Lynnie's life than what she was sharing with everybody, even her. She could sense something was missing but did not know what it was and wondered if Lynnie would eventually share this with her. Grace Elizabeth figured that if Lynnie wanted her to know then Lynnie would tell her.

Then it dawned on Grace Elizabeth; she wondered if Lynnie was missing Deb and just did not want to share how she felt about this just yet. Maybe Lynnie did not even realize she missed Deb, but it did show a bit in her expression. Rightfully, Lynnie should have strong feelings for this woman she called mom for so long. Grace Elizabeth wondered if she would be able to find Deb and bring her and Lynnie back together.

Grace Elizabeth and Lee were sitting outside while Mike and Lynnie were inside bonding and looking at pictures together. Grace Elizabeth figured now was the time to ask Lee what he thought about finding Deb for Lynnie.

"I know this is going to seem a little awkward, but I want to find Deb and bring her here for Lynnie."

"Can I ask why you feel so compelled to do this?"

"The expression that Lynnie had on her face was as if she were missing Deb when she was speaking about her."

Lee agreed and thought that was a good idea. Lee even suggested that if Grace Elizabeth wanted to find Deb that he would help any way he could.

He had some friends who worked for the local sheriff's department and he went for a walk to get some fresh air and clear his mind. He did not want anyone to know that he was placing a call to his friends asking for their help.

Lee did not have a whole bunch of information to give them about Deb, only her name and a picture that Lynnie had shared. He had taken a picture of Grace Elizabeth and Lynnie while Lynnie was holding the picture that had Deb in it. He emailed this picture to his friends at the sheriff's department so they had something to go on. While he was on the phone with the sheriff's department, they told him that Rick was in jail. The information that Lee had provided the sheriff's department to find Deb also showed Rick's information. Rick had been locked up for not paying child support and was in a jail in Florida.

Giving a little giggle, he thanked them for the information and made sure they had his cell phone number to call when they had more information on where to find Deb.

When Lee arrived back at camp, he shared the news of Rick being in jail with Grace Elizabeth. Neither Lee nor Grace Elizabeth was sure if Lynnie needed or wanted to hear about Rick being in jail right now, so they waited to say anything.

Lee wanted to make sure that the emotions did not shift about so much that everyone would be confused and figured it would be best to leave well enough alone for now.

Mike and Lynnie were still inside sharing stories, pictures, and catching up on all the years they had been apart. He realized that his sister Lynnie was a very intelligent person and appreciated her sense of humor.

Lynnie loved how Mike always had a smile on his face and was so happy. His smile lit up the whole room and she enjoyed Mike's love for God. He was a very grateful young man, grateful for all that he had and for his family.

Mike decided now was the time to share information about Annie with his sister.

"Hey sis, I have a fiancé; her name is Annie and she is truly my passion in life. We are planning to get married soon and we are both so excited. She is a schoolteacher and loves to work with children. She would like to meet you and asked if it would be okay if she came here. I told her that it was fine with me, so she should be here sometime today. She has been struggling all of her life, almost in the same way you have."

Mike stopped talking for a moment trying to find the right words.

"Annie lost her parents when she was young and has been in and out of foster homes all of her life. Her twin sister and she were separated when they were both very little. She has not seen her in a long time. She has been looking for her though and hopes to one day find her. Annie has had a lifetime of torment and despair, what seemed like unending abuse, and emotional torture. She made it her goal in life to work with children, especially troubled children; she could relate to them and could share in their sorrow."

Just then, Lee's cell phone rang. The call was from the Sherriff's office that Lee had called just a little while ago. They had news of where Deb may be and it was not far from where they were camping. The Sherriff's department was sending an officer out to identify this lady and make sure it was Deb.

"Grace Elizabeth. I received a call and they may have found Deb. They will confirm this and call me back. Hopefully she is not that far away from us."

Grace Elizabeth told Lee to go ahead and do what he felt comfortable doing, so Lee pardoned himself from the reunion and headed to the Sherriff's office.

Chapter Seven

Grace Elizabeth sat on the couch listening to Mike and Lynnie talking back and forth. They were sharing silly childhood memories with each other. She realized Lynnie was still showing some unresolved dismay on her face, but knew that Lee would have the answer with him when he returned.

After a short while, Annie arrived and pulled up out front. She got out of the car and headed for the motorhome. Lynnie was appalled and instantly furious! As soon as she saw Annie, she was convinced this was a set up.

"How could you do this to me! Why is she here? Get out of my way! I'm leaving!"

Mike and Grace Elizabeth just stood there looking at each other trying to figure out what was going on; neither could not believe how angry Lynnie had gotten or how furious she was.

Lynnie ran out of the motorhome and went to grab Annie, but Grace Elizabeth stopped her just in time. She was ready to fight and was not worried in the least who was trying to stop her. She drew back and lunged her fist toward Annie and Mike caught her and threw her to the ground. Annie ran into the motorhome crying, scared for her life.

When Mike realized he was still lying on top of Lynnie struggling to keep her under control, he was almost furious.

"What in the world is wrong with you? Why are you so mad? Would you just calm down! If you get yourself under control, I will let you back up!"

All Lynnie could do was struggle to try to break free of Mike's hold.

"That is not Annie, her name is Amy and she is married to my ex-husband Tim! I know who she is and I do not want to be anywhere near her! She took Tim away from me!"

Mike managed to get Lynnie under control and let her up.

"Why did you call her Amy? Why would you think any of us are lying to you Lynnie? No one here would do anything to hurt you Lynnie; you must know that."

Lynnie proceeded to tell Mike about the girl that Tim left her for and eventually married.

"Can I please get the box of pictures that are in the trunk of my car?"

"Yes, Lynnie you may."

Lynnie pulled out a picture of Tim and Amy from the newspaper when they were married and showed it to Grace Elizabeth and Mike. The girl in the picture looked just like Annie. Now Mike understood why Lynnie was so furious. Then it clicked! This was Amy, Annie's missing twin sister. Mike called for Annie, but she was too afraid to come outside where Lynnie was, so Mike went inside to her and showed her the picture.

"This is a picture of who Lynnie *thought* you were Annie."

He showed Annie the article from the newspaper. The picture was of Amy, Annie's sister that had been separated from her when they were little. They had finally found her!

Once everything was back under control and Lynnie apprehensively apologized to Annie, everyone sat down at the table to discuss how they could find Amy. Lynnie was not sure if she wanted to be a part of this since Amy may still be married to Tim and Tim was the last person Lynnie wanted to share the same air with again. Lynnie knew that she needed to help Annie find her missing sister, but was not sure how she would feel about seeing Tim again and bringing those all memories back to life.

Annie recalled some of the memories she had with Amy when they were little and she shared what she remembered.

"Amy and I were little when my parents died. They were killed in a terrible car accident and it left us alone. We were pushed around through the social service youth department from foster home to foster home, which was frightening and horrible every time we had to go to another home. The torture, the pain, the torment; all so hard when you are so very young. We never knew the true meaning of what having a family was like. It seemed like whenever we would get close with the family we were living with, social services would move us to another foster home, and we had to start all over again. It was not long before they took my sister away. They sent her to live with a family down in South Carolina and I was left here in Pennsylvania."

Annie dried her eyes from crying when the memories replayed in her mind.

"I never knew why they only took her and did not take both of us. I never heard another word from my sister after that. I never knew where she was until I was old enough to start looking for her on my own. The only information I was able to find was out that Amy had been placed with a family in South Carolina, but nothing more. No names. No address. Nothing. I hunted everywhere trying to find her and never could. I was never even close to finding Amy; nothing came up, ever."

Then Annie started crying again. She tried to hold back the tears, but just was not able to. Her heart was breaking all over again. Lynnie reached out and took ahold of her hand to comfort her. She could relate to how Annie was feeling and knew that no matter how she felt about seeing Tim again, She had to help find Amy.

Grace Elizabeth could sense that Lynnie was getting too overwhelmed by all the changes in her life and emotions she had been experiencing. She thought Lynnie needed some time to absorb everything.

"Lynnie, would you like to go for a walk and get some fresh air? It might help your nerves calm down a bit."

"Yes, that sounds like it would probably be a good idea. I will just take a walk down by the lake. I will be back shortly."

Lynnie walked outside and headed down by the lake. She did not want to go too far; she especially did not want to get lost. Lynnie saw a bench down by the water and thought that was a good place for her to go clear her mind.

Once she was far enough away, Grace Elizabeth, Mike, and Annie sat there in silence just astounded by the day's events. Grace Elizabeth was not sure if she should say anything to Mike about Lee being out to investigate if the Sherriff's department found Deb. Grace Elizabeth figured she would wait to say anything in case Lee was not able to come back with Deb.

Mike and Annie were discussing how they were going to locate Amy now that they had a recent picture and a basic idea of where she may be. They had decided not act on anything right now and just relax and free their mind for a while.

The silence was deafening in the motorhome when Lynnie returned a short while later. She was mentally exhausted and needed to lie down, so she headed for the back of the motorhome to lie on the bed and try to regroup from the day's events.

"Would you two mind going for a walk to give Lynnie some quiet time?"

Lynnie overheard Grace Elizabeth.

"Please, can you stay here? I do not want to be left alone. I will be able to rest better knowing you are all here."

Mike suggested maybe watching a movie or listening to the radio and Grace Elizabeth said that would be fine, so they turned on some light music. As the music played softly in the background, Lynnie drifted off to sleep.

In the midst of her snoring and the radio playing, Grace Elizabeth's cell phone rang. It was Lee; he was returning alone. The lady the police thought was Deb was clearly not her; although did fit the description perfectly. They were continuing their search and Lee wanted to be there with Grace Elizabeth.

"I will be there shortly. Is there any fresh coffee made?"

"I will make you a fresh pot of coffee and have it ready for you."

Lynnie heard the phone ring and reached for her own cell phone; only to realize it was not her phone ringing. She shrugged off the numbness in her shoulder and proceeded to get up from her nap. She asked Annie and Mike to sit with her at the table so the three of them could get the information together to find Amy, knowing this would help cheer up Annie. It was the least she could do for making her feel bad.

Sitting at the table and looking through Lynnie's pictures, Mike realized that she had been living a very hard life. He saw pictures of her run-down apartment that she once called home. He saw pictures of Lynnie with a bruised eye and she claimed that she had run into the door; he knew that the door was more like someone's fist and that was evident by the outline of the black around her eye. He noticed how skinny she was and malnourished she appeared. He also saw that she did not appear to have a smile on her face in most of the pictures.

He was able to find a picture that she was smiling in; the picture of her and her big pregnant belly. He managed to hold back the tears and not cry looking at the expression on her face when she saw that particular picture. She was obviously very devastated over the loss of her twins and he could respect this enough not to make any comments.

Mike was glad that he and Lynnie had been reunited and she could have a normal life now. He also appreciated seeing the difference in her then and now. It made him feel closer to her seeing her so vulnerable to life in her pictures.

Annie felt compelled to ask questions but stifled this until Lynnie was ready. She wanted to know about Amy and prepared herself to hear the worst. She knew that Lynnie did not have a good impression of Amy and could understand. She also realized that Amy was not the sister she was expecting to be reunited with; she was sure Amy had turned to a life of drugs and prostitution, and this upset her; she always expected her sister to be in a rich home, with rich parents, and living the finest life any kid could want. Now she realized that this was clearly nothing more than what she imagined.

Lynnie decided she would share the knowledge she had of Amy, even though she disliked her.

"I met Amy for a very brief time shortly after I found out I was pregnant with the twins. She worked at the doctor's office where I went to get my checkups; she was actually the receptionist there. She was a very pleasant, blond haired, green-eyed young lady who was very good at her job."

This was harder than Lynnie imagined it would be, but she knew she had to talk about her.

"Amy was a hard worker and was always busy when I went to the office. She had a charming demeanor and friendly personality. There was no wondering why the guys loved going to the doctor with their wives; they were only going to see Amy. She was a very pretty girl; very thin and had a large chest, like most guys like in a girl."

Lynnie realized she was holding her hands in front of her chest when she described Annie's chest size.

"I am not surprised that she caught Tim's eye; every girl caught Tim's eye. Tim was like a snake charmer, but he charmed women instead. Tim and I had run into Amy at the shopping center in town and she was alone that day with her car that had broken down. He offered to help get it running again and it all must have started then. There were evenings that Tim would be gone all night long and never come home until the next day. He even spent the weekend away on a couple occasions and never told me where he had been. Just said that he was out with the guys, like it was a get out of jail card he could throw around and be excused without me asking anymore questions. Rather than argue with him, I just let it go."

Rolling her eyes, Lynnie recalled the several times this took place and it upset her even more to think about it.

"Tim knew I was pregnant and my emotions were playing havoc with me and he did not want to argue with me either. Then one day, I went to my doctor's appointment earlier than what I was scheduled, which was okay because I was in the neighborhood anyway and it was easier than going home and then back down town again. I was sitting in the waiting room and the two of them walked in hand-in-hand. There were wedding bands on their left hands! They had gotten married over the weekend. I knew something was up with him, but never questioned it. He had taken his white shirt with for the weekend he was planning to spend 'with the guys'; he was such a lying, cheating, two-faced, bigot of a man."

Lynnie pounded her fist into the palm of her hand, and then brushed her hair back from her forehead.

"I was so angry when I saw this that I lost my temper. I was furious! There in the waiting room, I screamed at both of them and stormed out of the office. Not long after that, I started bleeding and it was downhill from there. I lost the twins shortly after that. I battled with the thought that 'all things happen for a reason' and was not sure if losing the twins was a good or bad thing."

Picking at the edge of a Kleenex, she was holding her hands, Lynnie felt the pain of that time all over again.

"I know I was pregnant with two children, girls, *my* girls. I lost them because I let myself get so stressed over Tim.

Losing them absolutely devastated me, it destroyed me completely. I hated life and fought with the realization that the twins were truly gone. I was not going to be a mother and convinced myself that Tim took that from me. He did this to me and I blamed him for how I felt. It took me a very long time to realize that I was a victim to Tim, another notch in his belt."

Lynnie was getting upset all over again and wanted this to be over.

"Tim was married to the sweetheart that all men wanted. He was married to your sister Amy. He did not care one single bit that I had lost the twins. It was almost as if he were elated that he was not going to have to pay child support and never shed a tear over his babies dying. His children were *dead* and he did not care. I sent him the pamphlet from the funeral home from the twins' funeral service that I had. I never heard from him again. I did see both of them together every now and then around town. I just kept my distance and tried not to interfere with them at all. I have the last address I had for Tim in my cell phone and I will give that to you. I am not sure if they are still there or not, but it is a good place to start."

Annie graciously took the address that Lynnie had written down and tucked it into her purse. She was reluctant to ask any more questions about Amy, even though she wanted to know more about her sister she had been missing for so long.

Lee arrived back at the lake a short time afterward. He had brought some dinner with him knowing that nobody was prepared to cook anything. The entire family sat at the table and joined hands to say grace before dinner. Mike led them in prayer with their heads all bowed down.

"Dear Lord, thank you for this reunion of my family. Thank you for bringing my sister Lynnie to us and us to her. Thank you for my loving wife to be, Annie. Thank you for the best parents in the world! Thank you for giving us this day! Thank you for this food, which we are about to eat. In Jesus name I pray, Amen!"

They all sat together as a family eating and letting the silence lead their minds to wander. Mike realizing that Annie's sister was another step closer to being reunited with them. Lynnie realizing that she had a family that loved her and missed her. She was grateful for this time they were all sharing together. Annie was thinking about Lynnie; how she struggled with losing the twins and knowing that Lynnie dealt with that by herself, with no one there to help her. Grace Elizabeth was thinking about her family all being together and how happy she was; how long she had waited for this day to come. Lee was grateful to see a smile on Grace Elizabeth's face and knew she was happy, even her heart was filled with joy.

Annie looked around at each of the people setting at the table with her and knew this was the right thing to do and she was sure that it would be okay with Mike.

"Lynnie, I have been thinking of asking you this question since Mike told me he was coming here to meet you. Would you be my maid of honor when Mike and I get married? I know it is short notice and I will understand if you don't accept. I would really appreciate having you there with us and being a part of our happy day. I would really love for you to be there with us if you can."

Mike grinned from ear to ear and Lynnie looked up with a smile on her face. She graciously accepted the offer and Grace Elizabeth felt her eyes welling up with tears, but she did not cry; she held her tears back.

Lynnie wanted to know when the wedding was going to take place and Annie told her that there had been no date set. She and Mike were just waiting for the perfect opportunity and time to come. They were so glad that Lynnie accepted that they wanted to get married before Lynnie went back to South Carolina. Now Lynnie had plans to make and a wedding to help with to add to all the emotions going through her. She was glad they asked her and graciously accepted this challenge; she knew she was up for it.

While they were finishing their dinner, Lynnie's phone rang; she did not recognize the number and figured whoever it was could leave a voicemail for her and she stuck her cell phone in her pocket. She did not want to interrupt the conversation between Annie and Mike about what flowers that Annie wanted to have at the wedding. Lynnie suggested that maybe some red roses would be appropriate and would go rather well with Annie's white dress. Lynnie heard the rhythmic tune her phone made when someone left her a voicemail, but figured she could check it later and went back to her conversation with Annie about flowers.

Lee and Grace Elizabeth sat there quietly while Mike, Annie, and Lynnie were feverishly making plans for the wedding. Mike and Annie knew it would not be an extravagant wedding and they did not want or expect that. The wedding was going to be very small and they were okay with that. They never wanted a big wedding and this fit into their plans perfectly. Grace Elizabeth was feeling a little tired so she went in to lie down while the others remained busy at work planning the wedding.

Mike decided that he wasn't helping matters by offering any of his suggestions about the wedding so he told Annie and Lynnie to work it out and let him know what they had planned. He sat on the couch watching television with his dad and enjoyed seeing the two girls working so well together. He knew this was a good sign and it made him feel good to see the girls so close.

Everyone was so overwhelmed with joy none of them wanted this day to end, but with all the different emotions combined with just finishing dinner, they were also getting tired.

Lee stood up to go grab another cup of coffee when he realized that Grace Elizabeth was sleeping quietly. Grace

Elizabeth snored, even if very lightly, but Lee knew she made a noise when she slept so he went in to check on her. When Lee opened the door, she was sitting on the edge of the bed, hunched over, and holding her chest. She was out of breath, gasping for air, and could not speak. Lee hollered to Mike, "Call 9-1-1 and get an ambulance here immediately. Your mother is having a heart attack!" He urgently wanted the ambulance to get there as quickly as it could.

Annie had been trained as an EMT in college when she was studying for her teaching degree and knew that she should try to give Grace Elizabeth an aspirin. Lynnie went to get the aspirin while Lee and Annie stayed with Grace Elizabeth.

Mike kept trying to get through on the phone but was not having any luck. His hands were shaking so bad that he could not get the phone to work. He stepped outside the motorhome and started shouting.

"We need help! Someone call an ambulance! My mom is having a heart attack! Hurry! Please hurry!"

A few short moments later, the Park Ranger pulled up out front and radioed into her dispatch center to send an ambulance to the park. The Park Ranger gave the dispatcher the location of the motorhome and stayed there until the ambulance arrived. After what seemed like an eternity, but was only a few minutes later, the ambulance crew finally arrived and loaded Grace Elizabeth up into the back, and sped off to the hospital with lights and sirens blaring.

Lee, Mike, Annie, and Lynnie all piled into Lee's car and they followed behind the ambulance. Lee was scared to death that he was going to lose his best friend; his loving wife; the woman he cherished with all of his heart. The tears welled up in his eyes, but he refused to cry. He fought back the tears with everything that he had in him. He knew he had to be the strong one so he could comfort his kids. He needed to stay strong on the outside while his heart was breaking into a million tiny pieces on the inside.

Mike was scared to death, so horrified that he could not even speak; he appeared to be in shock. Annie had a million thoughts running through her head and just could not bear to even think of what they were doing in the ambulance.

Lynnie was crying so hard she was shaking; she was absolutely devastated. She was not prepared to lose the mother she had just recently come to meet. Her eyes were red and swollen because she had been crying so hard.

After they emergency room staff had Grace Elizabeth stabilized, they allowed the family to come into her room to see her. The doctor asked them not stay too long, but could visit her for a little bit.

Lee was the first to go in Grace Elizabeth's room to see her. He was glad that she was able to smile at him. He knew that she was the only person in his life that could keep him going every day. She was the reason for his very existence. He knew that he was put on the earth by God to take care of her and she returned the favor by making sure he did his job and did it well too.

Mike soon peeked around the curtain with Annie holding his hand, the two entered next. Glad she was sitting up and talking; they had feared the worse and were prepared to see tubes and monitors with bells and whistles hooked up to her. They appreciated that she only had a heart monitor on and some oxygen to help her breath.

Lynnie was next to come in, but she waited quite a while before doing so. She had a tough time gaining her composure and the strength to go in the room. She fought back tears just at the mere thought of losing her mother and she just could not stop crying. She felt it would be best if she waited until she was able to go in there and see her mother without crying. She was also going to wait for someone to come out and give her an update; maybe that would help ease her mind.

The doctor came into the room to give everyone an update on her status, but Grace Elizabeth made him wait until all of the family was present and sent Lee out to get Lynnie.

When Lee found her, she was propped up in a corner looking out the window. She was watching the birds flying and the flowers swaying in the cool breeze; she was calmly gathering her thoughts and trying her best to calm down. He walked up to her and hugged her.

"Your mother is doing better. She is sitting up in bed and the physician wants to give all of us an update on her status, but your mom would not let him begin until you were there too."

Grace Elizabeth wanted her entire family in the room with her when the doctor gave them the news about her heart.

Arriving back at Grace Elizabeth's room, Lynnie hugged her mother and managed to control her urge to want to cry. She stood there waiting to hear what the doctor had to say.

The doctor came in with Grace Elizabeth's chart in his hands. He removed his glasses, folded them, and put them in his jacket pocket. Then he began to share the news they were all waiting to hear.

"I have to tell you; whoever found Grace Elizabeth so quickly and responded with the aspirin may have saved her life. She has a condition that we call angina, which means chest pain that occurs from a lack of proper blood flow and oxygen through the heart. We are going to give your mother a prescription of nitroglycerin or nitro as most people refer to it, and she is to take this when she feels this chest pain. She will place one pill under her tongue and let it dissolve. She can place one nitro under her tongue and repeat this again in five minutes if the chest pains do not resolve. This can be repeated up to three times only. In the event that she has chest pain again, someone will have to call 9-1-1."

The tone of his voice faded as Lynnie tried to let this moment sink into her mind without letting the tears run down her cheeks.

"The most common side effect of nitroglycerine is a headache and dizziness. We are going to observe her for a while longer to make sure she is safe and then we will make a decision about whether your mom can return home this evening."

Grace Elizabeth knew why she had this attack of angina. She was overwhelmed with meeting Lynnie and having her whole family together, but she would never let on to anyone this was the reason. She would confide in Lee when Mike and Lynnie weren't around and they could talk openly. She was certain that this was going to spoil everyone's day and she apologized to all of them for messing up their reunion.

Mike, Annie, Lynnie, and Lee all agreed that her health was more important than anything right now and that she did not need to think about anything; she just needed to get herself well. This reminded Grace Elizabeth that she needed to share her medical records with Lynnie and keep her up to date on her family health issues. She was tired from all the hustle and bustle and the medications that she had been given. She was comfortable enough that she fell asleep and rested for a short time.

The physicians all agreed that Grace Elizabeth could be released to go home. Lee was glad to hear that she had gained enough strength back that she did not have to stay in the hospital overnight. Mike and Annie went to get the car so Lynnie stayed with Lee and her mother.

Lynnie decided to wait out in the waiting room for them so Lee could help Grace Elizabeth get dressed. Lynnie made sure to tell him that she would be right outside the door and to let her know if they needed anything, no matter what it was.

Lynnie remembered that someone had called her cell phone earlier and left a voicemail. She decided that now would be a good time to check her messages. She dialed the number and entered her passcode. The system told her she had one message waiting and it was marked important. The message was from Amy. She said she found the number in Tim's box of things and wanted to let her know that he had been in a horrible car accident and was not expected to live through the night. He had been out drinking with his friends and passed out while he was driving home. The tone of her voice was all the proof Lynnie needed that Amy was not telling a lie. She left a call back number in case Lynnie wanted more information.

Lynnie felt terrible knowing that Tim was in such a potentially fatal situation. She really did love Tim at one time and they shared a past together, as well as the loss of their twins. She had to find out what was going on, but she needed to wait until the time was right to call Amy back. Grace Elizabeth's life was more important than anything was right now and Lynnie needed to make sure her mother would be okay, which was her top priority.

Mike and Annie returned back up to the waiting room after going to get the car ready for Grace Elizabeth to go back home. Lynnie wanted to let Annie know that Amy was distraught on her voicemail message, but just as she asked Annie if they could talk for a moment, Lee came pushing Grace

Elizabeth around the corner in a wheelchair. They were ready to get back to the motorhome.

Grace Elizabeth's color had returned to a normal shade of pink and no longer ashy-grey colored, and her spirits were perked up a bit that she did not have to stay overnight. They all left in one large group plundering down the hallway to the elevator. The ride back to Pymatuning Park was a quite thankful ride and the family was glad to all be together. They were all so thankful that their mother didn't have to stay at the hospital.

When they arrived back to the motorhome, they all agreed that Grace Elizabeth would have someone with her around the clock, without fail. Lee stated that he would not leave her side for any reason whatsoever. He was not about to lose Grace Elizabeth, especially if he had any control over the situation.

Mike, Annie, and Lynnie decided to go outside for some fresh air and to let their parents rest for a bit. They were sure they needed to relax and unwind after such a stressful ordeal. Annie asked Lynnie what she wanted to talk with her about at the hospital.

"Annie, my phone rang earlier, when we were all sitting at the table, and I let my voicemail get it. While I was waiting for Lee to bring mom out of her hospital room, I checked my messages and it was Amy calling me. She found my number in some of Tim's things. He is in the hospital not expected to make it through the night. He had been out with his friends drinking and was in a bad accident. She left a number for me to call her back and I want you to have the number. I wrote it down for you on this piece of paper. She did sound really upset up over the possibility of losing Tim and I am not sure if I can return a phone call to her now or not. Nevertheless, I know you are looking for your sister and I told you I would do my best to help you."

Annie took the piece of paper from Lynnie and was not sure what to even say to Amy. After all, it had been years since they were together, many years.

"Thank you Lynnie. I appreciate this."

Mike suggested that Annie call her sister might give her some hope when she was probably feeling like she did not have any. Although it may not be the best way to reunite with her after all these years, it was still as good a time as any.

Mike said they could go get her if Annie wanted to leave now. He was sure everyone would understand. She thought it would be best to wait and see how the phone call went first. She was going to sit on the park bench by the lake and give Amy a call now before she lost the number.

Annie dialed the number that Lynnie gave her and Amy answered right away thinking it was Lynnie calling her back.

"Amy, before you hang up I want you to know this is not Lynnie calling. This is your sister, Annie."

The phone went silent, as she knew it would. Then Amy broke the silence.

"Annie, is that really you?' How did you know where to find me? Where are you? Oh my goodness, I just am in shock I do not know what to say! Wait, you called me from Lynnie's phone, how do you know Lynnie?"

"Well how I know Lynnie is a whole new story that can wait for another time. How are you Amy?"

Annie continued to talk with her sister while Mike and Lynnie watched the expressions on Annie's face change from scared to a smile. Mike enjoyed seeing Annie with a smile on her face and knowing that she was talking with Amy made it all better. Even though he could not hear what they were saying, he was glad that they had been reunited after so many years had passed.

The lives of so many changed in just a few short hours. New mothers, brothers, fathers, sisters, friends, old memories, new memories, tragedy, trauma, heartbreak, and terror all poured into a few short days. There was more happening with this family than one person normally experiences in a full lifetime and they were all sharing these changes together.

Chapter Eight

Lynnie was headed inside to check on her mother. She knew that Mike and Annie would be a while on the phone with Amy. She also figured Lee would need a break or some fresh air, so she went in to make sure everything was still okay.

Grace Elizabeth tapped on the edge of the couch for Lynnie to go sit down beside her.

"I want to share some of my medical history with you. I know you are a healthy young woman, but just in case there may be a problem later in your life; I want you to be aware of what my medical background is."

Grace Elizabeth handed Lynnie a big folder packed with papers and other documents.

"This folder is for you to keep. It has some of my records from surgeries that I had and information that you may need one day. While you are glancing through there, be sure not to get too alarmed at what you read. I am healthy now and that is all that matters."

Lynnie took the folder from her mother and thumbed through a few pages.

"We do have a history of diabetes in our family, extending back to my grandparents as best I can gather. We also have a history of heart disease and yes, even I myself had a heart attack at a very young age. The cardiologist said that my heart had scar tissue in several areas. He also said that I shouldn't be too concerned; I was too young to have anything majorly wrong."

Lynnie couldn't help but wonder how young was too young to have a heart attack. It was serious at any age.

"A few years later, I was diagnosed with uterine cancer and had to have my uterus removed. My lab work has all been fine since then and I didn't need to have chemo or radiation. Thank goodness, I was able to have you and Mike first. I also have coronary artery disease, high cholesterol, arthritis, and fibromyalgia. I am not on any medication other than a hormone replacement patch after losing my uterus and being so young. I should also mention that I have quite an extensive history of cysts, all over my joints. I have them in my brain and on my brainstem too."

Lynnie was shocked to hear all of this. She always thought her mother would have a perfect bill of health; little did she realize this was not the case.

"The doctors at the Cleveland Clinic in Ohio told me to have followup scans of my brain for a while to make sure they did not grown in size or move. I never went back to the neurologist after they told me the cysts were there. I did not figure there would be a reason to keep having tests done on something that has the potential to come and go as easily as a cyst. I had to have several removed from my ovaries and they finally took both ovaries out not too long ago."

This sure was a lot for Lynnie to absorb. She never realized that her mother would have so many different things wrong and wondered how many things she could have that were genetic.

"The only *major* health problem I have is the inability to handle stress. I do not take stressful situations very well, as you can tell. My body dislikes stress of any kind and shuts down when I am exposed to it for any length of time. One final thing you should know Lynnie, I have scar tissue on my brain. When I was a little girl, your

Grandma Lisa would hit me on the head with a hard plastic hairbrush every time she brushed my hair. I had the long brown curly hair and the best-looking pigtails! She would hit me on top of the head with that plastic brush if I even so much as grimaced when she pulled my hair when she was pulling it back into a ponytail. It really hurt too, so I quite often ended up crying by the time she was done brushing it. If I spoke up and even uttered 'ouch' she would hit me twice as hard. I was to sit there and not say a word, nothing more."

Lynnie could never imagine having that happen to her. How horrible that her grandmother had to be so hateful and mean.

"I had seizures from the head trauma and had to take Dilantin when I was little. For the majority of my childhood, I had to sit inside; I wasn't allowed to play with the other kids. Your Aunt Karen came and went as she pleased. I was inside cleaning most of the time, not allowed to be a little kid. I was not allowed to spend the night with friends and they were never allowed to come visit me."

Lynnie sat there listening to her mother speak with a puzzled look on her

131

face and wondering how anyone could be so cruel.

"Your Grandma Lisa even saw me have a seizure one time and screamed at me to get up off the floor, quit acting like an idiot, and to go sit in the chair. Karen was so mad at Grandma Lisa for that and she helped me get up. Your Aunt Karen knew that the seizures were no game and was scared every time I had one. She always assumed that the seizures would eventually kill me."

Lynnie could hardly believe what she was hearing. How could a mother do something like this to their child, to treat them with such hate was appalling.

"Even though I had the seizures from being hit in the head, this never stopped Grandma Lisa from hitting me with the brush or the belt, whatever she could get her hands on to use was good enough for her. I even wiggled my bottom front teeth one time when I was just a little girl, you know how kids do, and Grandma Lisa backhanded me knocking the teeth out of my mouth."

"Oh my gosh! How cruel! I just cannot imagine someone being so mean, just downright mean and hateful."

"Such a cruel and vicious person she was, but I always did my very best to try to please her. It was never good enough, but I still tried."

Feeling pressured and more worked up after telling Lynnie these things from her past, Grace Elizabeth decided that was plenty for now. She could finish another time.

"Enough of that for now, I need to relax and calm myself down a bit; maybe rest my eyes for a little while."

She thought it would be best to relax and take a few deep breaths. Lynnie would be here for the next few days so there was no reason to try to jam everything into a couple of days.

Lynnie just sat there amazed at the torture Grace Elizabeth had been through her whole life. Mental and physical torture from the one person who was supposed to love and protect her. She could almost feel the pain and sadness that her mother felt while listening to the stories.

She knew what it was like to grow up in a broken home and how so many different things can happen to just one person. She herself knew what it was like to try to prove your love to the one person who kept rejecting you, over and over. Lynnie also knew what it was like to never do anything right in the eyes of someone you only wanted to love you.

Lynnie was lying on the couch with Grace Elizabeth when Mike and Annie came back inside. Annie had obviously been crying and Mike was trying to console her. Lynnie listened to part of their conversation as they sat there contemplating what to do next. It appeared as if Amy did not want to leave Tim's side just yet; she wanted to remain there as long as she could. Annie was heartbroken to think that her sister could pass up the opportunity to be together after they had been separated so long ago. She felt like a complete fool for calling Amy and Mike was trying to help calm her down.

Lee was watching the race on television holding onto Grace Elizabeth's hand. He really did love her and Lynnie felt blessed that he was in her life too. He was the glue that had held her mother together all these years.

His cell phone started to ring and he glanced at the screen to see who it was before answering.

"Stay with your mom, I need to take this call."

The call was from the Sheriff's department and he did not want to have a discussion with Lynnie setting there in case the news was not good.

A short time later, he came back out into the living room and returned to his seat holding onto Grace Elizabeth's hand. He never mentioned the call or anything about it; almost as if it never took place.

The entire family sat together in the same room, but each had their own world spinning around in their head. The information that had been shared over the past couple of days was quite a bit more than any of them could each handle and they all decided to just enjoy each other's company, in silence. Just be a family occupying the same space, without adding more to it.

After a short while, Grace Elizabeth woke from her nap and she was hungry. She was going to make dinner for everyone and wanted to make sure she had everything she needed before starting.

The menu was grilled steaks and sweet potatoes, with some zucchini on the side. As she checked her cupboards for the brown sugar to put on top of the sweet potatoes, she realized that she did not have any.

"Mom, Annie and I can go to the store to get you a bag of brown sugar. Lynnie would you like to ride along?"

"Yeah, sure. I'll ride along. A change of scenery would do my heart some good I think."

Once they had driven away and the car was out of sight, Lee told Grace Elizabeth about the call he had received earlier.

"While you were asleep, I got a call from the department. It appears they may have found Deb. I asked them to make sure it was really her before they called me back. They are checking into this and will let us know what they found out. If the person they found is Deb, Lynnie will be very upset. It seems they found this woman in a hospital in Texas. She is on the same floor where they have the cancer patients who are palliative care only and not expected to live much longer."

Knowing that they really needed to wait for the Sherriff's department to call them back with proof of the woman they thought may be Deb; Grace Elizabeth could not bear to think of how Lynnie was going to react to the news and how devastated she was going to be. Lee assured his wife that if the woman truly was Deb and accurately verified to be the same Deb they were looking for, they would all fly to Texas so Lynnie could see her before she passed away; all pending on her wishes of course.

Grace Elizabeth stated that she wanted to go if it was Deb, even if Lynnie decided against it. Deb had raised Lynnie and Grace Elizabeth wanted to thank her for taking such good care of her daughter. She wanted to thank Deb face-to-face and not through the words of a letter or over the telephone. He called the department back and asked if they had any verification yet, and the officer stated that they would call him back as soon as they had more information.

A short time later Mike, Annie, and Lynnie returned with the brown sugar they had gone to the store to get. Lynnie had also grabbed some snacks and some marshmallows for roasting over the fire later.

Lee and Grace Elizabeth were busy preparing the steaks to put on the grill, wrapping the sweet potatoes in foil and buried them deep into the fire so they would be ready in time to eat with the steaks. They were all sitting around the picnic table drinking coffee when Lee's cell phone rang. Grace Elizabeth and Lee met eye-to-eye hoping it was the news they were waiting for.

Grace Elizabeth knew they would need a little time to prepare Lynnie for the tragic news and for a quick trip to Texas. He again excused himself from everyone's presence so he could take the call privately. When he returned to join them, he asked that Grace Elizabeth go for a walk over to the water and sit on the bench with him while the coals were building up nicely in the fire.

"I must say, the Sherriff's department has been right on top of our request. The officer they sent to the hospital has verified that the woman lying in the hospital bed is in fact the Deb we are looking for; the doctors have given her only a few short days to live. It appears that she has breast cancer and the treatment they gave her did not work. She is hooked up to all different kinds of machines and falls asleep quite frequently. She has some difficulty breathing and they say it is because of the cancer spreading into her lungs. We need to tell Lynnie so she can let us know what her intentions are. If we need to leave sooner than expected, we can get the arrangements taken care of now so there will be no delay."

Grace Elizabeth felt horrible knowing that Lynnie would be heartbroken at the loss of Deb. She was not exactly sure how to approach Lynnie with the news, but knew she had to and did not have any time to waste either. Deb did not have the time for anyone to wait; her days had already been dwindling away.

Grace Elizabeth and Lee decided they would let Lynnie know of their plan to find Deb for her and tell her of the news they had just received. They would include Mike and Annie too, wanting the whole family to know what was happening so they could all be there for Lynnie to support her.

They had decided that Grace Elizabeth would be the one to tell the others about this and they walked back over to the fire where everyone was sitting. She sat down beside Lynnie and put her arm around her shoulder pulling her close to her side.

"I have something I need to tell you Lynnie. I want all of us to be involved in this conversation because it is not going to be easy for any of us."

Mike and Annie sat down and joined the conversation after Grace Elizabeth motioned for the two of them to sit down with them.

"Lee and I were trying to see if we could locate your momma Deb for you, as a surprise. Hoping maybe, she was somewhere nearby and we could bring her here to see you. Lynnie, we have been in touch with the Sherriff's department who has been helping us try to find her and they have called with some news that is going to break your heart. Lynnie – your momma Deb is in a hospital in Texas. She is in a palliative care section not expected to live much longer, a few days according to her physicians. Deb is being treated for breast cancer and the treatment is not working."

Lynnie could not hold back her tears anymore and let them flow freely down her cheeks. She was sitting there speechless and started shaking, and was obviously very distraught. Grace Elizabeth held onto Lynnie, hugging her, and helped comfort her while she was absorbing the news of her momma Deb. Mike and Annie sat quiet as well, not knowing what to say to her. They knew who Deb was, but never met her personally; they were more upset for Lynnie.

"We can make arrangements to go see Deb at the hospital if you want to go."

Lynnie shook her head and agreed that she would like to be there for Deb.

"I have every intention of thanking Deb as well for taking such good care of you Lynnie and raising you so well."

Lynnie realized she needed Grace Elizabeth more than ever now. She needed the security of knowing that her mother would be by her side through all of her grieving. She did not want to hurt her, but felt she needed to be there to say her final goodbyes in person and asked Grace Elizabeth to be there with her. Lee said he would take care of the booking the flight and get a room reserved near the hospital. Mike and Annie agreed to stay behind and take care of things while the others went to Texas.

When they landed in Austin, Lynnie was overcome with a feeling of sadness that she never knew existed. She was at a hospital to see the only mother she had ever really known - with her birth mother by her side. She wondered how Grace Elizabeth was handling this and was concerned about her heart. She did not want her to be under too much stress. She suggested that when they arrived at the hospital to see Deb that she go in alone, first. She had some things she wanted to say to Deb, but did not want to make Grace Elizabeth feel out of place. She understood and agreed to wait until Lynnie had a chance to speak with Deb privately. She knew the facts and appreciated the bond between the two.

Grace Elizabeth was still trying to make peace with herself after Lynnie's arrival in Pennsylvania and having the attack of angina made her realize that she needed to watch her own stress level. There were quite a few things going on and she needed to make sure she paced herself appropriately. She did not want to end up in the hospital, she only wanted to soak up every moment of life that she could with Lynnie. She had a lot of catching up to do with her and did not want an overload of stress to be the reason she missed this chance.

Lee and Grace Elizabeth walked over to the chairs in the waiting room and sat down, while Lynnie proceeded to walk down the hallway towards Deb's room. She stopped at the nurse's station to make sure she had the right room and asked if she could get an update from the nurse before she went into her room. She was sure she wanted to do this alone, but was not sure if she had the strength.

While she stood there listening to the nurse tell her about Deb's condition, all she was able to hear were words like *"short-term"*, *"she is not feeling any pain"*, *"she is resting comfortable"*, *"matter of time"*. It was all a jumble of words to her and she could not fit the puzzle together in her mind. She was starting to fall apart and needed to find a way to hold herself together, even if just for a while longer. She decided to take her time and walk slowly to her room recalling some of her favorite childhood memories that she shared with Deb. The memories were playing like a movie reel in her mind at high speed. She was trying to focus on keeping her composure when she reached the door to Deb's room. Lynnie silently told herself, *"this is it, keep yourself under control, Deb does not need to see you cry, keep yourself together girl, you can do this!"*

Lynnie opened the door to her room and Deb was lying there sleeping. She looked so thin and her face was a pale ashy color. Her cheeks were sucked in on both sides, she looked like a skeleton with skin over top of her bones; she looked so frail. She had an oxygen tube in her nose to help her breath and a pain pump to administer morphine when she needed it at the push of a button. She had a whole room full of flowers and pictures that her friends and family had sent to her. She sure had a lot of love and support by the looks of all the gifts in her room. Lynnie wondered why no one was there to see Deb and why she was there all alone.

Deb opened her eyes and saw Lynnie standing there. She smiled the biggest smile on her face. She was so happy to see Lynnie that she started crying and her heart monitor started making noises until a nurse came into the room to see if everything was okay. She reached out for Lynnie, wanting to hug her and hold the little girl she had been missing for so long. She had lost touch with her over the years and Rick would never let Lynnie see her. He refused to allow the two of them to have any communication whatsoever. She was so glad that Lynnie was there. It had been a very long time and she hugged Lynnie tighter. She knew she had to tell Lynnie she was sorry for leaving, even though she was forced to go. Lynnie was only a little girl then and would have never understood what happened. She hardly understood it herself, especially not enough to explain to a child.

"Oh my sweet little Lynnie, how I have missed you. I tried for so long to find you and ran into brick wall after brick wall. Your father asked me not to contact you or anyone in your family. I was told to leave and never look back. Your father reassured me that he would never let you and I see each other again. I am so glad you are here now. How did you know I was here? Did the doctors tell you about my cancer? I only have a few days left to live according to them. I get so tired and fall asleep so very easy. I just can't get my legs to work enough to have the ability to walk anymore. The treatment took the strength from my body and left me unable to take care of myself. It is better that God take me and give me a new life. I would prefer not to stay here on Earth and live in torment any longer. God will take care of me and I will live with those who had passed before me. I will be able to see my mother and father again. I will be able to watch over you without anyone telling me that I can't, not your father or your Grandma Lisa. No one can stop me! I am so glad that you are here. How did you know I was here?"

Lynnie realized that Deb was in the final stages of her life and it hurt her to listen to the woman she called mom throughout her childhood repeating herself, unaware of what she was saying. She had been rambling oddities that made no sense and Lynnie knew that she had lost all control and was not long for this world. Lynnie wanted to make sure Deb knew just how grateful she really was for raising her.

"Momma Deb, oh how I have missed you! I want to thank you for being my mom and raising me with so much love. You were there to fix my skinned knees, you were my driving coach when dad took my training wheels off my bike; you were my teacher; you were my friend most importantly. You also gave me the gift of love by making sure that I knew who my birth mother really was."

Lynnie felt herself getting choked up with her words and tried to slough it off, but just couldn't.

"Momma Deb, Grace Elizabeth brought me here to see you. We have spent the past two days together. She and I arranged to meet at the lake in Linesville, which is in Pennsylvania; we met there after all these years. She was so happy to see me. I was so excited to finally get to see her again. It had been so long. Oh, guess what else? I have a brother! His name is Michael; they call him Mike, and he is studying to be a minister. He is engaged to a very nice girl by the name of Annie. We were planning their wedding when Lee, that is Grace Elizabeth's husband, my stepfather, received the call that the Sherriff's department had located you. They were going to surprise me by finding you and bringing all of us together. He never expected that they would find you here in the hospital. They are here with me, waiting outside your room. Grace Elizabeth wants to come in and speak with you. I will have her come in and see you and then I will be back afterwards."

Lynnie left Deb's room quietly, walked past the nursing station, and headed straight for Grace Elizabeth. Lynnie knew that it would not be long and Deb would pass away. She could just sense it after seeing her lying there.

Grace Elizabeth knew this day too would come eventually, but that did not make it any easier for her. How was she going to thank another woman for raising her child? She appreciated Deb's gratitude for sharing her memory with Lynnie and sneaking some of the gifts to her that Rick wanted thrown out. Deb overcame the torment from Lisa that she was sure had to be hard on Deb. It was hard on her too. She entered Deb's room and Deb had already fallen back asleep. She was looking around at the flowers and cards people had been sending in to Deb, wishing her well. She was glad that she was there to speak with Deb face-to-face, as humbling as it was.

Deb grunted a weird noise and opened her eyes; she gasped for air, but was able to catch her breath. She looked over to see Grace Elizabeth standing there. She really wanted to hug her and tell her thank you for bringing Lynnie there to see her. She reached her arms out welcoming Grace Elizabeth.

"Thank you, Deb."

The two women respected each other for being Lynnie's mother, each in their own way. Grace Elizabeth knew Deb was tired and needed to rest, so she did not hesitate any longer. She was determined to thank her, and that was her full intention.

"Hi Deb. I am so sorry to finally be seeing with you under these conditions. I always figured it would be you and I sharing coffee together, and pictures of Lynnie growing up. I never would have guessed it would be in a hospital. I am so sorry."

Grace Elizabeth could feel herself getting worked up, but she knew she wanted to do this. She convinced herself to keep it together long enough to get through this.

"Deb, I have to tell you thank you. Thank you for raising Lynnie to be the fine young woman she has become. Thank you for sharing who I was with her. Thank you for being the mother I could not be during that time. Some children have broken homes and never know one parent or the other for whatever reason. Our Lynnie knows both of her mothers. She is such a great girl. She speaks so very highly of you. I could never repay you for being the mother you did not have to be to my daughter. I owe you so much, Deb. Thank you, thank you."

Deb looked up into Grace Elizabeth's eyes and could see how sincere she was. She could see the tears welling up in her eyes and the sense of love for a child that only a mother has. She knew she would see her one day and was glad that they had the opportunity to see each other before the cancer took her life. She wanted to tell her thank you as well.

"Grace Elizabeth, it is sure good to see you after all of these years. Lynnie told me you and Lee had been trying to find me to surprise her. How very thoughtful of you! She sure is a good girl. I knew she would do okay after Rick threw me out into the street. I tried to keep in touch with her, but Rick and Lisa would not allow us to even talk. I am so glad that she was finally able to reunite with you too. She loved the cards you sent her and the gifts; she had no idea they were from you until later in her life of course. I knew she would figure it out soon enough. For me to tell her then would have been sure terror for her if her father ever found out. I am so glad to see you Grace Elizabeth. Thank you for coming here to see me and bringing Lynnie here for me. We sure have quite the daughter; she is the joy of my life."

Deb was nodding off to sleep while she was thanking Grace Elizabeth for bringing Lynnie in to see her. She knew she better let Deb rest a while, so she left the room to go out and see how Lynnie was holding up.

Lynnie and Grace Elizabeth sat there reminiscing the last few days together. They were so glad they had this opportunity to share together and Lynnie was so appreciative to Lee and Grace Elizabeth for bringing her here to see Deb.

Lee glanced over to Lynnie with a comforting smile that really touched her heart.

"It is almost as if a broken circle of life has been made whole again. First you and your mother, Grace Elizabeth, were together. Then, you and Grace Elizabeth were separated. Next, you were joined with Deb, now you and Grace Elizabeth are back together, and you are both here with Deb. God works in mysterious ways and while we may not always understand His reasoning, He has a bigger plan for all of us. We can be grateful to Him for these days we are all sharing together. It is His plan that the puzzle fit together the way it does."

Lynnie nodded her head in agreement. She was replaying the words Lee had just spoken over again in her head and realized he was right. The broken circle of life had been made whole again, but her heart was still felt heavy over Deb's condition.

Lynnie knew that Deb would be passing away soon and wanted to be there when it happened. She wanted to make sure they had the chance to see the doctors when they came in to do their rounds and have another chance to check in on her. She knew that Deb did not want to die alone; no one does. She also knew that she stood the chance of having some less than desirable people show up at the hospital to see Deb while she was there. She was also determined not to let that bother her; she was there to spend Deb's last few moments with her and was not there for any other reason.

Lynnie felt confident that anyone that came to the hospital would be to see Deb and nothing more or so she hoped anyway. She leaned over and laid her head on Lee's shoulder, and stared out the window into the night sky. After having such a strenuous day, she wanted to stop her mind from whirling in circles. She had been to see both of her mothers in the hospital in just shy of a full twenty-four hours. How could one person go from having no one in her life to having all of this confusion? She was not sure how that happened to her, but she was sure glad it did.

Lynnie knew she had to start lightening her stress load some too or she would be the next one having medical problems. She did not want that to happen, so she decided it would be best to just let her mind slow down and relax while she sat there with Grace Elizabeth and Lee in silence.

After spending the night in the waiting room at the hospital, Lynnie was growing more curious of Grace Elizabeth and wanted to know all she could about her. She knew that Deb was the lady who raised her when she was little, but was not her mother. She wanted to get to know *her* family. After spending so much time with nothing much to do other than wait and think, she grew more fond of Grace Elizabeth and Lee. Could she ever be close enough to Lee to have a relationship like a true father and daughter? Did God bring them all together so she could share in the true meaning of love? The more she wondered the more she wanted to know.

Lynnie figured the only way she was ever going to know would be to seek the truth for herself. She knew she could trust what Grace Elizabeth was telling her and she knew that Lee would be there to support her mother through any of her tough times. She figured now would be a good time to ask questions since they were all there and it just seemed appropriate. She decided it would help lighten the mood as well. She asked Grace Elizabeth to share more of her past.

Lynnie heard more about Michael and his younger years. Grace Elizabeth even shared with Lynnie that Michael had a hard time growing up not knowing his sister. He knew about her, but she was not there and he could not figure that out. The kids at school had their brothers and sisters at home with them, but his sister was not anywhere that he could see her. While they were sitting there talking about the past and sharing more memories, the doctors came into the waiting room and shared that Deb was in the final moments of her life and if they wanted to go into her room to be with her now would be the time.

Grace Elizabeth and Lynnie walked into Deb's room together. She was sad to see Deb lying there lifeless in every way, but the heart monitor was still blipping, very slowly. Grace Elizabeth knew that she was going to have a difficult time enduring the loss of Deb.

After Lynnie and Grace Elizabeth had been in Deb's room for only a short time, the heart monitor blipped slower and slower until the line that was once pointed had gone solid signifying that Deb's heart stopped and she had died. The sound of Deb's last gasping agonal breath would be carved into Lynnie's mind forever, but she was glad that Grace Elizabeth was there with her. She cried while holding onto Deb's hand; thanking her for being her mother while she was growing up. She was very appreciative to her for being such a caring person and she was glad to have known this wonderful lady she called momma Deb.

Grace Elizabeth was also thanking Deb for helping Lynnie grow into such a fine young woman. She thanked Deb for being there through all of Lynnie's growing up milestones and was grateful that the two could share in these things together.

Grace Elizabeth and Lynnie spent quite a while in Deb's room after she had passed. They were sharing in a true bonding moment and holding onto the past for memory-sake. They had so much to learn about each other. They had only spent the last few days together, but Lynnie already felt like she had known Grace Elizabeth all of her life and she owed that to Deb.

Grace Elizabeth felt she missed out on so much of Lynnie's growing up that she felt compelled to spend as much time as possible with her and really never wanted her to leave, ever again.

Grace Elizabeth, Lynnie, and Lee were getting ready for the flight back to Pennsylvania. While they were gathering all of their belongings and making sure they had everything, the phone in their hotel room rang. It was the front desk telling them a piece of mail had arrived for Lynnie and it looked very important.

On her way out, Lynnie walked up to the front desk and asked for the piece of mail they had called her about that was there for her. It was a large yellow envelope with

Lynnie's name handwritten on it. Inside there were rings and jewelry that had belonged to Deb and a handwritten letter that Lynnie took the time to read.

My dearest Lynnie:

If you are reading this letter, then it means the cancer has finally won. I truly do not want to leave you like this, but obviously, I did not have a choice. Cancer is not forgiving to anyone for any reason.

I have sent you this letter to let you know there is a small inheritance that will be coming to you. It is not much money, but a little bit. I also have a couple of things that I feel you should know.

First, I am glad that I was able to know you and your mother Grace Elizabeth. You were both a very important part of my life. I may not have shown it all the time, but I really did cherish you. Raising you was the highlight of my life. I know you were not my own flesh and blood, but I never let that stand in the way of how I felt about you. I loved you as if you were my own daughter. I truly regret not spending more time with you after your father and I separated. He would not allow me to have any contact with you whatsoever. I did find you once, but he would have killed me had he known that I watched you playing in the playground at school. I knew he was never going to let us be together again, so I had to be careful in my every attempt to see you. Nevertheless, you were then and still are my shining star and I love you.

This is where it gets tricky...your father Rick and your Grandmother Lisa know that I am ill and not going to survive this terrible disease. They will be expecting you to come here to see me. Please be careful and protect your heart from their attacks, and focus on yourself, make your life better. Please do not let either of them knock down the world you have built for yourself. You are a strong and courageous girl; I am afraid they could try to persuade you to change your mind about wanting to find your real mother. Please, just follow your heart and ask God to guide you towards her and He will lead the way.

Please know I love you Lynnie – take care of yourself and may God bless you my little girl.

Love,

Momma Deb

Lynnie stood there reading the letter over and over, with tears rolling down her face. She could not believe her momma Deb was really gone. Deb's death just sunk into Lynnie's heart and stirred around tearing her up bit by bit. This was harder than she expected it to be and she really needed Grace Elizabeth right now.

Grace Elizabeth and Lee came walking around the corner carrying all of the suitcases and bags that they had packed up. Grace Elizabeth saw Lynnie standing there, reading a piece of paper, and crying; deciding it was best to let Lynnie have some time to herself, she helped Lee pack the bags into the taxi. When she walked back into the hotel to check on Lynnie, she saw her still standing there reading the same paper she had in her hand before.

"Can I help you with anything?"

Lynnie grabbed ahold of Grace Elizabeth and cried on her shoulder for what seemed like an eternity. She just stood there holding onto her and let her take all the time she wanted.

She knew this was a difficult time for Lynnie and it broke her heart to see her cry. She wanted to make her feel better, but she was not sure how to go about doing that just yet.

"Ladies, we need to get going if we are going to catch our flight back."

Lee held the door open for them as they all piled into the taxi for their trip back to the airport.

They were all eager to get back to Pennsylvania and put an end to these last few days of grieving. Lynnie watched out the back window of the taxi knowing that Deb was still there and she would never see her again. This really upset her and she cried again as they rode to the airport.

When they arrived back in Pennsylvania, Lee had to go back to work for a little while and Grace Elizabeth and Lynnie were taking some much needed down time together. They had spent the past couple of days shopping and catching up with each other.

Lynnie had left Grace Elizabeth's address and phone number at the front desk of the hospital where Deb had passed away.

She felt it best that if there were any belongings or other items that were Deb's, she did not want it going to South Carolina when she would not be there to receive them. She wanted Deb's remaining possessions to be sent to Grace Elizabeth's address where it would be safe from the temptation of thieves who would be on the watch for it.

There were packages that arrived for Lynnie with the return address of the hospital and each contained pictures of her and various little trinkets that Deb wanted her to have. There were more cards that Deb never had a chance to read to her that Grace Elizabeth had sent when Lynnie was little. Both Grace Elizabeth and Lynnie sat and read those together. Some of the cards still contained the money she had sent for her. How amazing that after all of these years, the cards remained untouched and unopened.

Lynnie appreciated Deb even more after receiving these pieces of mail. She had been hanging on to these for so long and was obviously in no hurry to pitch them out or open them.

After a few short days passed by and everyone had a chance to regain their sanity,

Lynnie and Grace Elizabeth each had remembered they still were in the midst of planning Mike and Annie's wedding and needed to continue on with the details. Lynnie called Annie to see how her plans were progressing. She was glad to have Lynnie back helping her with the wedding. They decided they would go back to Pymatuning State Park where everyone was still camping.

They wondered if having the wedding at the park would be a problem. They could go to the beachside where the pavilion is and have the service there where the guests could sit at the picnic tables and the view there was amazing too. They had stopped in town to see the Clerk of Courts to get a marriage license on their way through the small one stop-sign town. The preacher of Mike and Annie's church was willing to go anywhere they wanted or needed him to perform the service. In a couple days, they would be married and begin their new life together. They had been dating for quite a while and were ready to settle down in the eyes of God and be a legitimate married couple. Lynnie and Grace Elizabeth had been downtown shopping and returned back to the campground to see that Mike and Annie had returned.

Lynnie and Annie were discussing the wedding details when Annie decided there would be no theme. This was going to be a regular black and white, genuine wedding. Friends and family were coming in as they received their invitation and were planning for a perfect day.

Lee and Grace Elizabeth offered to supply the food for the occasion and they were very appreciative. Since they were getting married at the campground they did not figure anything other than hot dogs and burgers would be appropriate, but Lee suggested steak and chicken grilled to perfection. He even offered to do the grilling and make sure everything turned out delicious for their guests. Grace Elizabeth offered to arrange the flowers and suggested using flowers from the park as place settings for each guest to take home as a memento of the special day. Annie thought that was a great idea and offered to help her arrange the place settings.

Lynnie offered to do the picture taking. She was already skilled in photography and wanted this to be her gift to the couple. Annie was thankful for her eagerness to take pictures, even though she was maid of honor, technically speaking.

She was planning to set up the tripod to hold the recorder during the ceremony while she maintained her position of maid of honor for the couple.

Everything seemed to be falling into place and they were excited about their special day that was fast approaching.

Everyone was busy with their own task and helping where they could in an effort to make sure everything would be perfect for the wedding.

When the day had finally arrived, Mike and Annie were very happy. The friends and family were starting to fill their seats and the ceremony was about to begin. Lee asked for everyone's attention and the preacher began the service.

Dearly beloved, we are gathered here today to witness the union of Mike and Annie in Holy matrimony.

It is said in Genesis 2:18-24 - The Lord God said, "It is not good for the man to be alone. I will make a helper suitable for him." Now the Lord God had formed out of the ground all the beasts of the field and all the birds of the air. He brought them to the man to see what he would name them, and

*whatever the man called each living
creature, that was its name. So the man
gave names to all the livestock, the birds of
the air, and all the beasts of the field. But
for Adam no suitable helper was found. So
the Lord God caused the man to fall into a
deep sleep; and while he was sleeping, he
took one of the man's ribs and closed up the
place with flesh. Then the Lord God made a
woman from the rib he had taken out of the
man, and he brought her to the man. The
man said, "This is now bone of my bones
and flesh of my flesh; she shall be called
'woman,' for she was taken out of man".
For this reason, a man will leave his father
and mother, be united to his wife, and they
will become one flesh.*

*I have known Mike and Annie for a
couple of years now and know they are quite
suited to be husband and wife. I am very
honored to be performing this service for
them today and share in their new life with
them.*

*Now, Annie, please repeat after me -
I, Annie, take you Mike, to be my wedded
husband. To have and to hold, from this day
forward, for better, for worse, for richer, for
poorer, in sickness and in health, to love and*

to cherish, until death do us part. I hereto pledge you my faithfulness.

Mike, please repeat after me – I, Mike, take you Annie, to be my wedded wife. To have and to hold, from this day forward, for better, for worse, for richer, for poorer, in sickness or in health, to love and to cherish until death do us part. I hereto pledge you my faithfulness.

Mike placed Annie's ring on her finger and said, "Annie, I knew this day would come. Thank you for being my best friend. I love you." Annie smiled and said, "Mike, I love you too" and she placed Mike's ring on his finger.

I now pronounce you man and wife. Mike, you may kiss your bride, Annie.

Grace Elizabeth was so happy, she started crying, and Lynnie walked out of the picture to get the recorder to continue filming her brother's special day. Lee was grilling the meats, but he was watching the service and had a smile on his face with tears in his eyes too.

They were so happy that Lynnie was there with them to share their wedding day. Mike's life could not get any better as far as he was concerned. He had everything he could ask for right there with him, including a new wife.

The guests were all holding their own conversations and the children were all playing and running around the park. Mike asked for the attention of the adults so he could share some words with them.

"I have something I want to share with you, but I need everyone's attention."

Once the conversations stopped and Mike had everyone's attention, he introduced Lynnie to the crowd.

"I want each of you to know who Lynnie is and I want each of you to welcome her into your lives. Lynnie is my sister who was viciously taken away from my mother when she was a little girl. The story is a personal one and I will not go into detail, but I would like to introduce my sister to you. Her name is Lynnie and she is here taking pictures for us today. Just know that she will be here with us now as part of my family. She is my sister, my friend, and I have waited a very long time to get to know her."

Mike held his wine glass in the air to solidify an acceptance cheer from the crowd.

Each guest was eager to make their acquaintance with Lynnie and show their gratitude. The preacher even shared in welcoming her to the family and whispered in Lynnie's ear.

"I would be happy to assist you with any counseling if you need it."

"Thank you."

Grace Elizabeth was busy talking with the guests while Lee was paying attention to the grill and making sure everything was coming along nicely. The day of celebration was coming to a close, but no one wanted it to end, especially Mike and Annie.

Chapter Nine

Lynnie knew she needed to be returning home to South Carolina soon. She had things she needed to follow up on there and work that she needed to submit so she could have some money in her bank account. She also knew that Grace Elizabeth and Lee would be eager to get back home too. Mike and Annie were moving in together before going back to work again on Monday. Lynnie also needed to get back to her somewhat *normal* life.

She knew she had to tell her mother her plans to go back to South Carolina and she knew that Grace Elizabeth was going to try to talk her out of it. She however was prepared for this and felt loved knowing that someone actually wanted to spend time with her.

"Mom, is there anything else that you can think of that you may want to share with me? Health problems? Stories about your life? Anything? I am thinking I need to get back home to South Carolina and I wanted to see if you had anything more you wanted to share with me before I leave."

Grace Elizabeth was hesitant to say anything, but Lee suggested she had better tell Lynnie about a few more things from the past; things that she knew no one else would tell her. Lee walked into the bedroom and returned with more photos and another envelope that he handed to Grace Elizabeth. With Lee's encouragement, she shared more with Lynnie.

"Lynnie, there are a few more things I need to share with you. These photos here are of your brother, Terry. He was the child born to your Grandmother Lisa and your father Rick. The two had an affair shortly after Rick and I separated many, many years ago. Your Grandma Lisa was pregnant with Terry when your father and Deb started dating. Terry lived a short life, but he was full of energy and very outgoing. He was playing with a gun at your Grandma Lisa's house and it went off shooting him in the head. Terry died instantly; he only lived to be eight years old. These are a few pictures that I have of him and I wanted you to know that he was your brother."

Lynnie took the pictures and thumbed through each of them, taking the time to look at Terry. She was shocked to hear that her father and grandmother had an affair; even more stunned to realize that they had a child together. Hearing this made her feel sick to her stomach, but she did not let these feelings show to Grace Elizabeth. She knew that her father Rick and her Grandma Lisa were evil people, but never figured they would do something this horrible. Grace Elizabeth shared more pictures of Terry and Lynnie together as very young children. She did not remember him; she was too little to remember much at all.

Grace Elizabeth continued to show more pictures and stopped when she got to a batch that had a rubber band wrapped around them holding them together. These pictures were horrific and she was not sure she wanted to show them to Lynnie, but knew she had to.

"Lynnie this next set of pictures that I need to show you is very disturbing. I really prefer not to show you these, but know that I must. If you are to have the full story of who you are and the history of your life, you need to see these pictures too."

Grace Elizabeth removed the rubber band from around the pictures and showed them to Lynnie. They were pictures of a little girl being molested by her father Rick. The camera had been hidden in the bookcase to figure out how the little girl was getting so many bruises.

Lynnie took the photos and realized that she recognized the little girl; this was the little girl that Deb used to babysit. Lynnie and this girl played together and basically grew up together. Her name was Tammy. She was Lynnie's best friend and then one day this little friend just disappeared. Lynnie never heard from her again and never saw her again. She often wondered what ever happened to her, but being little the memories were short-lived.

Grace Elizabeth grabbed Lynnie's hand before she showed her the rest of the photos from that bunch.

"Tammy died a very horrible death and it was in the papers."

There were newspaper clippings and articles mixed in with the photos that Grace Elizabeth handed to Lynnie. She made sure she told Lynnie that the pictures were very gruesome and heartbreaking, but she wanted Lynnie to know the truth.

Lynnie took the photos and newspaper clippings and opened up the article that was folded around the biggest paper clipping. The photos inside made Lynnie set back in her seat and grab her stomach. The headlines read, "*Young girl dies from hanging.*" Lynnie started reading the article to get some background information. The writer stated that Tammy had been strangled by a cord to a lamp and that the cord had obviously been cut by a sharp object. The assumption was that the cord was put there for Tammy to be "accidentally" hung by. The death was ruled accidental, but everyone knew better. It was homicide, but no one could prove who the killer was. Grace Elizabeth knew because the lamp once belonged to her. It was taken away from her when she was little by her mother, Lisa.

Grace Elizabeth knew that Lisa played a role in this because Rick had been showing Tammy too much attention, even if it was harmful attention at his molesting hands. This did not matter to Lisa and she would be sure to stop the meetings between Tammy and Rick; no matter if it cost the little girl her life. The investigators could not prove that it was Lisa who had cut the cord, so she was released from being their prime suspect. They never did find who cut the cord from the lamp; there was not enough proof to arrest a suspect, so they had to rule it accidental.

Lynnie sat there in silence for quite some time. Soaking in the news of her brother that died from shooting himself in the head. She finally knew what happened to her childhood friend Tammy after all these years. Destructed by the hands of her Grandmother Lisa; the woman *was* truly the devil. How could one woman be so evil and hateful? Lynnie was astonished to think this evil person was her own grandmother.

Grace Elizabeth wanted to make sure that Lynnie was okay after seeing the photos that were wrapped up and tucked away for so long. Knowing that she was close with Tammy at one time, Grace Elizabeth knew that she would take seeing those photos and reading those articles very hard. Lynnie did not really know who her brother Terry was, but she was still bothered by the thought of losing him and never getting to really know him, after all, he was her brother.

Lynnie was starting to feel overwhelmed with all of the changes that had been taking place since coming to Pennsylvania to meet Grace Elizabeth. She learned about having a brother, Mike who was wonderful in every way. Annie was such a sweet girl that Mike would have a great life being married to Annie. Deb's passing hit her hard and Lynnie missed her. Lynnie knew that she would never see Deb again and she was grateful that God brought them together and cherished every memory she ever had of her.

The greatest thing to happen to Lynnie was meeting her mother Grace Elizabeth. Lynnie was so very thankful to have such a great mother and she loved her. She loved getting to know her and she loved the family she had now.

Lynnie knew she would have a hard time leaving to go back home to South Carolina. It had taken her so long to find her mother and get to know her that Lynnie never wanted to leave her again. Lynnie suggested that she and Lee come to South Carolina and learn more about her life there, and share in some of her memories that she had built over the years. Lee made the suggestion of driving the motorhome down to South Carolina so Grace Elizabeth and Lynnie did not have to part ways anytime soon. He could take some vacation time and would do the driving. Grace Elizabeth and Lynnie thought that was a great idea and made plans to prepare for the trip.

Mike and Annie were staying behind again to keep an eye on things at home in

Pennsylvania. They really did not mind. They both had to work, so it fit for them to just stay there.

She was both excited and a little nervous to share Charleston and the life she had there with Grace Elizabeth and Lee. She wanted her mother to know everything about her that she could share.

Lee arranged to take some vacation time and cleared his schedule for the next few weeks. Grace Elizabeth had her work with her, but she too took some much needed vacation time and set her work aside for the trip she was taking with Lynnie. She was eager to learn about Lynnie's life in South Carolina; her friends, hangouts, hobbies, and everything she could fit into the time she had available. They would be leaving in the morning and had to make sure they were stocked with food and ready to head down the road.

The next morning, everyone was prepared to head south to take Lynnie home. They had rented a trailer to haul Lynnie's car behind the motorhome so she would not have to pay fees to have it transported back. Everything was in its place in the motorhome and Lee pulled out of Pymatuning State Park headed for Interstate

95 south for Summerville, South Carolina, where Lynnie lived.

They drove to a town called Breezewood, Pennsylvania; from there they picked up Interstate 70 east and from there to Interstate 270 east and on to Interstate 95 south.

There was an RV resort in Roanoke Rapids, North Carolina that Grace Elizabeth and Lee had stayed at before and was the perfect stop when traveling down the east coast. The resort was a nice spot that had all the hook-ups they needed for the night and had easy access back onto the Interstate the next morning.

Once they made it to the resort, Lee was outside hooking up all of the connections so they could have all the amenities of home with them.

The ladies were walking the paved road loop around the resort looking at the different RVs parked there. Some were permanent sites and the people lived there year-round. The other sites were for visitors. The resort had cabins that could be rented out. There was also a Laundromat and a swimming pool there. They had putt-putt golf up front as well. The evening sky was a beautiful shade of blue and the birds were enjoying every last drop of sunshine before the dark grey evening sky covered the blue.

When Grace Elizabeth and Lynnie returned from their walk to the spot where the RV was parked, Lee had everything all set up for them to enjoy the evening and rest before getting back on the road in the morning. He built a campfire in the fire pit and made some hot dogs for dinner. Lynnie was enjoying this time she had with the both of them. The RV made it easy for them to travel together and have everything they needed right at their hands.

After eating dinner, Lynnie went inside to grab a quick shower before pulling out the couch bed. Lee and Grace Elizabeth were putting away the things outside and preparing to come in for the evening. They were sitting at the table when Lynnie came out from her shower.

They were all sitting at the table talking when Grace Elizabeth's cell phone rang. It was Mike and he had Annie on speakerphone. The tone of his excited voice told them this was going to be good news.

Annie shouted in the background, "I'm pregnant! How great! I am so excited! We just received the news from my doctor and we had to share it with you first."

Grace Elizabeth and Lee just looked at each other, both with big smiles on their faces. Lynnie was just as excited and had tears of joy in her eyes.

"What wonderful news; we are so happy for the both of you. My first grandchild!"

Lynnie could not help but think of the twins she had been pregnant with and miscarried. She had mixed emotions; both sad and happy, but was happy for Mike and Annie. She was also saddened to have the memory of losing her children so vivid in her mind again. She could never let her sorrow show in front of Mike and Annie; she did not want them to be burdened by her memories.

After the call was done and everyone had a chance to congratulate Mike and Annie, Lynnie headed for bed to get some sleep. Lee and Grace Elizabeth had the same idea. They would all be getting up early in the morning to complete the rest of their trip to Summerville and Lynnie was anxious to get back home.

It was six o'clock in the morning when Lee woke up and he was already in the shower when Grace Elizabeth and Lynnie smelled the coffee that had just finished brewing for them. Grace Elizabeth walked out into the kitchen and grabbed three coffee mugs from the cupboard, and proceeded to pour coffee for everyone. Lynnie woke up feeling refreshed and ready for the day.

Lee was outside getting everything picked up and ready to get back on the road. Grace Elizabeth and Lynnie were inside putting things when Lynnie shared her sorrow with Grace Elizabeth.

"I am glad Mike and Annie are pregnant. I really want the best for them. I must admit though that it hurts my heart and reminds me of the twins. Am I ever going to get over the pain of losing them?"

"The only way to recover from such a traumatic time is to ask God to help you through it. He is there and waiting to lead the way for you. All you have to do is ask Him. Remember, all things happen for a reason and while that reason may never be known to us, God knows the answer."

Lynnie accepted her mother's advice and knew the only way to come to terms with her troubled memories would be to let go of the past and commit to working on a better future for herself. She knew this was not going to be an easy thing to do, but also knew she could endure the path if it helped her overcome. She was compelled to make sure she healed from her wounded past and move on with her life; even if it was not an overnight battle she could win.

Once everyone was showered and everything was back in its place, Lee maneuvered the motorhome around the road towards the exit of the resort. Interstate 95 was straight ahead and in a matter of minutes, they were traveling southbound again. They rode in silence enjoying the scenery that the southern interstate shared with them that morning; bright blue skies, loads of sunshine, and a smell of wildflowers in the air. It was not long before they crossed in South Carolina. Lee stayed on Interstate 95 heading south for approximately six hours, until he arrived at exit 86-A where he turned onto Interstate 26 east heading towards Charleston. Lynnie was starting to feel a little more like she was at home, once she realized that it would not be long before they would be at the exit in Summerville.

Once Lee saw exit 199A on Interstate 26, he knew that was where he needed to be. He exited off the interstate and headed for Lynnie's apartment. Grace Elizabeth had been trying to locate an RV park where they could stay while they were in South Carolina. She called all of the closest parks she could find, but they were all filled. Lee stopped at a gas station to fill up and Grace Elizabeth went inside to see if anyone had any idea of another park for them.

"Do you know of any motorhome parks that are nearby where we could stay? It seems the closest ones are all filled; a private park would be great, but if there is nothing like that near here a public park would be absolutely fine too."

The clerk replied, "My uncle has a private RV lot in North Charleston, not too far from the highway. I can call and see if he has anything available for you."

"That would be wonderful, thank you so much!"

A short time after Grace Elizabeth walked back outside, the clerk came out and told Lee that her Uncle did in fact have a spot open. He wrote down the directions and thanked the clerk for her help.

The lot was in a private park near the military base and close to shopping. Grace Elizabeth was pleased with the location and Lynnie said that she was familiar with the area. They decided to make this little park their home for the time they were going to be in South Carolina with Lynnie.

Chapter Ten

Once Lee parked the motorhome, Grace Elizabeth started making the inside more comfortable for them. She opened the windows to let some fresh air in and soon closed them. The southern air was getting hotter by the minute, so she turned on the air conditioner instead to cool herself off.

Lynnie was outside helping Lee get her car from the trailer. They were going to return the rented trailer down the road a bit and rent a car from the store next door. They both decided to get that accomplished while Grace Elizabeth was preparing the inside of the motorhome for them.

They arrived back shortly and parked both vehicles in the extra lot the park owner set aside for the cars. While they were still outside, Lynnie called Luke.

"Hi Lynnie, are you back home yet?"

"Yes, we just made it back to North Charleston today. We are at the little RV Park near the military base. Did you want to stop by and meet Lee and Grace Elizabeth?"

"Sure, I am not busy this evening. How about after I close the store?"

"Good, I can't wait to see you! Then maybe you and I can go for dinner together? Better yet, why don't I pick you up and we can all go to dinner this evening."

"Sounds good. See you later tonight. I have to run; we are busy today. I am glad you're back." Lynnie was glad to be back too.

After they were done outside, they went inside to see how Grace Elizabeth was.

"Mom, I want to take you and dad…" catching herself when she called Lee dad. She was stunned, not to mention Grace Elizabeth and Lee.

"Oh my goodness, I cannot believe I just called you dad, Lee. I am so sorry. I hope I did not offend you."

He was shocked, but not bothered by her calling him dad. In fact, he liked it.

"Lynnie, I am not bothered at all. You can call me dad, if you want too."

Lynnie went back to her statement she was trying to make previously.

"I am taking you and dad to dinner tonight, my treat. We are also picking up

Luke at six and he will be joining us this evening. I want you both to meet him."

Lynnie decided to drive over and check on her apartment while Grace Elizabeth and Lee were settling into the park. She wondered how Amy was holding up with Tim being in the hospital and decided to give her a call. Lynnie dialed the number Amy left for her and waited for Amy to respond; instead, she received Amy's voicemail and decided to leave a message for her.

"Hi Amy, this is Lynnie. I am back in Summerville. Let me know if you need anything. I will be here for the next several days, so whenever you get the chance; there is no rush. Thanks. Bye."

When Lynnie arrived at her apartment, she was glad to be back. She never realized how much she missed her home and belongings. She had a box full of mail that needed to be sorted out and cleaning that needed her attention. She put the box of mail on the table and sat down on the couch to let her mind absorb all of the changes she had been through over the past few weeks. Lynnie's mind was racing and she only wanted it to slow down and not be so busy. She wondered how Luke was going to like her parents and vice-versa. She knew Luke would be welcomed by Grace Elizabeth and Lee, but would they "*like*" him? Or find him dull and boring? She let her mind wander off in her thoughts and fell into a relaxing sleep. She could not have been asleep for more than ten minutes when her cell phone rang. She woke up unsure of where she was and it took her a moment to realize that she was home.

The number displaying on the cell phone screen was the number that Amy left for Lynnie to call her back. She answered the phone with a yawning "hello." Amy was on the other end of the line crying,

"Lynnie? This is Amy, are you there?"

"Yes, I am here. How are you Amy?"

Before Lynnie could get any more words out of her mouth, Amy started crying.

"Amy, are you okay?"

"Tim died this morning. There was nothing the doctors could do for him. He was so badly torn up from the accident that he laid here and died. The doctors gave him pain medicine, but there was nothing they could do to treat all of his injuries. He's gone! I just cannot believe he is gone!"

Lynnie felt crushed at the news of Tim dying. She had been married to this man at one time and was pregnant with *his* twins. How could this be happening to her, she wondered.

"Amy, do you want me to come to the hospital and just be there with you?"

"No, it will not do either of us any good to sit here without him. I am going to go home and take a shower. Lynnie, do you have Annie's phone number? I'd like to talk to her if you have it."

Lynnie was not sure if she should be giving out Amy's cell phone number, so she told Amy she would find it and let her know. Once she hung up from talking to Amy, she called Annie to tell her that Tim died and to let her know that Amy wanted to talk with her.

Annie hung up from talking with Lynnie and immediately called Amy. She wanted to help reassure her that everything was going to be okay for her. She also wanted her to know that she was very sorry for her loss. Even though she had not seen her sister for so many years, she still felt connected to her and wanted to make sure she was going to be okay.

Lynnie figured she better get ready to go pick up Luke from the store. She wanted to see him before picking up Grace Elizabeth and Lee for dinner.

When she arrived at Luke's store, she was welcomed with a huge big basket of flowers and Luke with a great big smile on his face and his hands stretched way out inviting her for a hug. Lynnie was glad to see Luke and hugged him tightly while she admired the flowers sitting on the counter waiting for her.

"I am glad you are back home. How was meeting Grace Elizabeth?"

Lynnie was dumbfounded to think that she had not even talked to Luke since meeting with Grace Elizabeth and had to catch him up on everything that had happened since she went to Pennsylvania.

"She is an amazing person, Luke. She was so glad to see me! We talked for quite a while. We spent time catching up with each other. I learned a lot about the people in my family who I assumed were good people; little did I know they were not good people at all. Oh, and best of all, I have a brother. His name is Mike and he married Annie while I was in Pennsylvania. Annie is Amy's sister...can you believe it? Sure is a small world, huh."

Luke just looked at Lynnie and tried to absorb everything he had just heard. He giggled a slight snarky giggle and grabbed Lynnie up again to hug her.

"We better get going since we have to go up to Summerville, North Charleston area."

Luke turned his blinking "*Open*" sign off, set the security alarm, locked the door, and headed for the car.

On their way towards North Charleston to pick up Grace Elizabeth and Lee, Luke asked Lynnie how *she* was doing. She told Luke about Deb. She also told him how Grace Elizabeth tried to bring Deb to her while she was there; little did anyone realize she was dying in a hospital. She also told Luke that she had found out some pretty traumatic things that had happened to her mother during the time after she was taken away. She also told Luke about being lied to by her Grandma Lisa and Rick. She was struggling with the proverbial question of *why*. Why would anyone treat their own flesh and blood so badly. Why would a person who gave you life, want to take that very thing away from you? She was determined to find out the answer to the question. She wondered if Grace Elizabeth had any other information to share with her and if so, maybe she needed to wait before she went digging any deeper into the past.

She shared with Luke the true story about Rick and Grace Elizabeth separating. She also shared with him the stories she had heard of Terry, her brother; the son of her Grandma Lisa and father Rick, dying from a "self-inflicted" gunshot wound. She shared Tammy's tragic story, about being molested by Rick and her suspicious death by suicide from a lamp cord. He sat there amazed at what he was hearing. He had never heard such a confusing family saga before.

""Lee said something to me that stuck in my head. He said that a broken circle of life had been made whole when Grace Elizabeth and I met up again after so many years. I will never forget. It is a perfect description of how our lives had been a complete circle when I was born;

then how our lives were torn apart shortly thereafter, breaking the circle; and now we are back together again and the circle is no longer broken. It is round and whole again."

Nodding his head, Luke agreed with Lynnie that her broken circle of life had been made whole again.

"I hope the circle stays round and never breaks apart again. I bet you are happy to have your mom back in your life and everything out in the open."

"I am glad that Grace Elizabeth and I are back together again, but I wish I did not have to hear some of the things she said to me. I am glad she told me, I was looking for the truth, and she told me; do not get me wrong, but I did not want to hear some of it. Maybe we should change the subject and try to think of happier thoughts before we get back to North Charleston. I do not want mom to think that I was crying and carrying on this whole time."

"Where do you want to go for dinner?"

"I think we should go to that little restaurant on the corner that I like, the one with the really good fried chicken; oh man what is the name of that place?"

"Jestine's?"

"Yes that the place. Maybe we should call and make reservations?"

"Lynnie, they do not take reservations there."

It was obvious to her that he missed her and was glad she came back home. She missed him as well, but really did not have the *time* to miss him per se.

When they arrived back at Grace Elizabeth and Lee's motorhome, he was nervous about meeting them. She tried to convince him they were down to earth people and he didn't need to worry.

When Lynnie pulled up out front Grace Elizabeth and Lee came outside, ready to meet Luke. Lynnie gave Grace Elizabeth a look as if to say, "*yeah he is nervous, but he will be okay*". Luke walked up to Lee and extended his hand. Lee shook Luke's hand noticing a firm, strong grip. Grace Elizabeth was next and he was so nervous his hands were sweating. She grabbed ahold of him and hugged him rather than shaking his hand.

"I am sure glad to meet you young man. I hope you are taking really good care of our Lynnie. She means the world to me."

Luke looked Grace Elizabeth in the eye with an expression on his face that he was serious.

"I would not hurt her for the world. She is my best friend and I never want to see her hurt, ever."

Lynnie introduced Luke to Grace Elizabeth first, "Mom and dad, this is Luke. Luke, this is my mom, Grace Elizabeth and this is my new dad, Lee."

Lynnie had her arm around Lee, who had his arm around Grace Elizabeth, who had her arm around Luke, who had his arm around Lynnie forming the perfect circle. Lynnie chuckled when she realized and said to herself... *This is a perfect circle and not broken. I wonder if this is truly what life is all about.*

Chapter Eleven

It was not long before Lynnie realized that time had been passing along for her and Luke. She had become reacquainted with Grace Elizabeth after being apart for so long and she was wondering if she wanted a family of her own. She knew that she had some unanswered questions that she needed to pursue and wanted Luke to be there for her during these times. She just was not sure if she was ready to love that deeply again. She also was not sure if she wanted to chance getting pregnant again either. If she were to lose another baby, she would never be able to live with herself. Losing her twins was one of the hardest times in her life and she just was not prepared to face that tragedy again. She decided to wait and talk to Luke to get his opinion. After all, he was the other half of her now and it was the right thing to do.

She also still had not been able to locate her Grandma Lisa. She had questions for her grandmother that she wanted the answers to. She knew it would not be easy to get the truth out of her or her father Rick either one, but knew she had to satisfy her own mind and find them. She wanted to confront them face to face with what she had learned over the past few months. She also wanted to watch their body language when they answered her questions. She decided that she might have an easier time finding her Aunt Karen to use as a route for finding her Grandma Lisa.

She started the hunt for her Aunt Karen online; she searched Google, Facebook, and Twitter, all coming up empty handed. Then she decided that maybe her Aunt Karen had a different last name now and that she was not going to be able to find her until she figured it out. She struggled trying to figure out how to find her father or her Grandma Lisa either one. Then she remembered that Lee heard Rick was in jail for not paying child support. She picked up the phone to call Lee and ask if he could help her.

Grace Elizabeth answered the phone when it rang.

"Hi mom, how are you today?" Is Lee around anywhere?

"I am fine dear, hold on just one moment and I will see if he is still here."

When Grace Elizabeth came back to the phone, she told Lynnie that Lee had gone out while she was lying down taking a nap. He left a note saying he would be back later that evening and he could be reached on his cell.

"Is everything okay Lynnie?"

"Yes, mother. Everything is perfectly fine. I will not bother Lee if he is busy. Can you tell him that I called please?"

Lynnie hung up the phone and sat back down at her computer to try to see if she could find her Aunt Karen again. She entered the last known address she had for her Grandma Lisa into Google to see if she could get a close up view of the houses on Main Street where Lisa lived. She wondered if she would be able to see vehicles or people outside using the zoom-in map. Lynnie figured that she did not have anything to lose by searching every way she knew how. When Luke got home that evening, Lynnie told him what she was doing.

"I am going to try to find my Grandma Lisa and my father Rick. I want to know why they lied to me all those years. I want to know why they did not tell me about Terry and Tammy. I want to know why my mother was treated so badly. I just want to know *why*."

Luke hugged her knowing that this was tearing her up inside. He tried to find ways to help her cope with her past and tried to find ways to help her handle the emotional stress she had been under. He just wanted her to be happy. If finding her Grandma and her father Rick made her happy, maybe he better help her that way and not try to change her mind. He knew he would not be able to change her mind completely about getting her answers from Lisa or Rick; although he did feel compelled to tell her how he felt.

"Lynnie, I wish that you could find Lisa and Rick and get the answers you are looking for. If you can't find them, maybe you need to wait and let them find you."

Lynnie was sure they would not even be looking for her.

"Did you ask your mom for help Lynnie?"

"I do not want my mom to be hurt anymore by these vicious people. I would rather take the blunt of the abuse and confront them myself than to see my mother hurt by them again."

Luke understood what she was saying and asked her if she had talked to Lee about any of this. Lynnie told him she had left a message for Lee to call her back. She was also sure that she needed to say something to her mother about what she was doing. She was going to have to say something before Grace Elizabeth started asking questions. She also did not want to lose the trust that she and Grace Elizabeth had in each other by hiding things from her. She just had to figure out *how* to tell her what she was doing.

After what seemed like forever, Lee called her back.

"Lynnie is everything alright? What is wrong?"

"No Lee, everything is fine. But, I do need your help with something. Are you free to talk for a moment?"

"Yes I am, do I need to be alone or can your mother hear our conversation too?"

"I prefer mom not hear anything, just yet. I will eventually tell her, but not right now."

"Ok, I am outside by myself now. Lynnie, what is going on?"

"I am trying to find Grandma Lisa and Rick. I need to resolve the pain I still have from them. I am having a difficult time forgiving them for what has happened to mom and I need the closure to move on with my life. I remembered when you and mom were trying to find momma Deb for me and you found out that Rick was in jail for not paying child support. Do you know if he is still in jail and if he is, where?"

"He was in a jail in Florida if I recall, but I will try to confirm this for you. Lynnie, are you sure you want to do this? Are you sure you want to relive the past and all that pain again? I understand that you need the closure to heal, but the pain is going to hurt and really hurt bad before everything is all said and done."

"Yes, I know, but I need to do this for me and for my mom. She deserves all the best in the world and I want to help her heal from this nightmare too."

Lee agreed that he would help her find Rick and Lisa, but he also told her that if Grace Elizabeth asked he would not lie to her and she appreciated his honesty with her mother.

After a few more days had passed with Lynnie not finding anything out online and Luke helping diligently, even at the store, to find Lisa and Rick; Lee called her back. He had information about where Rick was.

"I have an address to the prison where Rick is. Now I can give you this address, but you have to promise me you will not go here alone. Lynnie, I am very serious. The prison that Rick is at is a very dangerous place and I do not want you to go there alone. I can go with you or Luke, but someone *has* to be there with you."

Lynnie agreed and said that Luke knew what she was doing and they were trying to find Lisa and Rick together, so he could go with her. Lee agreed and gave Lynnie the address.

"You can find Rick at the Florida State Prison in Starke. The address is 7819 Northwest 228th Street in Raiford, Florida, and the zip code is 32026. Please Lynnie be very careful. This prison has been known to have dangerous inmates; Ted Bundy was there at one time until they executed him in 1989. Just make sure you keep yourself safe that is all I ask." Lynnie gasped slightly when she heard Ted Bundy had been at Starke.

She wondered what Rick had done to go from a jail to a prison now.

"Do you know why Rick is in a prison now and not a jail?"

"Unfortunately, I don't know. I only know he is there. I can find out for you if you want to know, but it may take some time."

"Yes, I would like to know why, if it is easy enough to find out. There is really no need to pursue if it starts getting difficult, but I would like to know."

"I have to go now, but thanks for calling. I will talk with you later."

Lynnie figured that Grace Elizabeth was nearby and Lee wanted to get off the phone before she started asking too many questions. She took the information that he had given her and started researching the

Florida State Prison online. She wanted to know a little about this place before she and Luke went there. While she was researching the prison, she thought about Rick and Tammy. How could a grown man molest a small child like Tammy? The pictures she had seen burned in her mind as she recalled each of them. What was he hoping to gain by hurting a little girl? Whatever the reason, Lynnie knew she was glad that he was in a prison and the reason no longer mattered to her.

Since asking Lee for his help, Lynnie felt compelled to tell Grace Elizabeth what she was doing. She did not want anyone getting upset if she did find Rick and Lisa. She knew she had to tell her mother, but she just did not know how. Then she realized the reason really did not matter; she just had to tell her mother how she felt about her Grandma Lisa and Rick. Grace Elizabeth would know the reason why and this was her hope.

She called Lee to let him know that she had decided to tell her mother everything. He was glad to hear this and asked her if she and Luke wanted to have dinner that evening. She said that would be a good idea and she could talk to Grace

Elizabeth then and it would be out in the open for all four of them to share in the quest together.

Lynnie called Luke at the shop and told him they were going to dinner with Lee and Grace Elizabeth that evening. She also told him that she was going to tell Grace Elizabeth about her plans to find Rick and Lisa so there were no secrets between them. He agreed that would be a good idea.

`That evening at dinner, she knew the time was right to tell Grace Elizabeth.

"Mom, I have to let you in on something. Please do not be upset, but I want you to know so there are no secrets between us. I am looking for Grandma Lisa and Rick. I need to get some sort of closure from them, from my past. I need to heal from my past so I can go on with my future. I know that I can never forgive them and expect everything in my life to be normal, but I need to be able to move on and not dwell on my past so much. The only way I can do this is to confront them and forgive them, face to face."

Grace Elizabeth looked up and met Lynnie's eyes with hers. She knew Lynnie was sincere and knew too that she did need to move on from the past. They all needed to heal from the hurt.

She thought about what Lynnie said for a couple moments before responding.

"Lynnie, I am glad you shared this with me. I am not upset with you by any means. I am glad you are trying to heal and move on from the past. I truly hope that you find what you are looking for. I also know how you feel and admire you for wanting to handle things so maturely. Maybe we can work on this together and help each other heal. I can help you find Rick and Lisa. Would that be ok? I really want to help you Lynnie."

"I would love to have your help. I must admit that I am concerned about your health. What about your heart and the stress you will be under?"

"I promise to watch my stress level and will pay close attention to my heart. Please, just let me help you Lynnie."

Lynnie agreed that she would love to have her mother's help and accepted her offer.

In the meantime, Lee looked at Luke and nodded; a nod that appeared to Lynnie to be a nod of approval. Lynnie thought this was odd, but did not ask any questions. Shortly afterward, the waitress came out with a bottle of wine and poured everyone a glass and the music started playing in the restaurant, a calm soothing sound.

"I would like to make a toast."

He held his wine glass up, as did Lynnie, Lee, and Grace Elizabeth.

"I would like to make a toast to everyone sitting here at this table. We have become so very close and have learned to appreciate each other for our own uniqueness. We have become friends and family, bound tightly together by the past while reaching for the future. I could never imagine spending my life with a more wonderful family than we have here and now."

Lynnie started to get a little emotional with Luke's kind words and wiped the tears from her eyes. Just then, Mike and Annie came walking around the corner and joined them at the table. Lynnie knew something was up and it had to do with the nod that Lee gave to Luke. After all of the hellos were said and hugs of welcome were given, Luke nodded to the waitress who brought out an envelope and handed it to him. He handed the envelope to Lynnie and asked her to open it. Inside the envelope, there was a piece of paper. She took the paper out and he asked her to read it out loud.

The paper had these words written on it…

Lynnie, I love you very much. I want to spend the rest of my life with you. I want to share all of my hopes and dreams together with you. I want to wake up every morning with you lying right there beside me. I want to see your beautiful face looking at me and making every day worth waking up to. I want to make you my wife. Lynnie, will you marry me? Wait, before you answer, there is more.

Lynnie, now with tears flowing freely down her cheeks was sobbing, continued to read the paper out loud.

Lynnie, this restaurant that we are in this evening now belongs to Grace Elizabeth and Lee. They have decided to stay here in South Carolina with you and me. Wait, there is more…

Mike and Annie have moved here as well. Mike has received his Masters of Divinity degree and will be pursuing his career here in Charleston. Mike has something to give you. Wait there is more...

Mike held his closed hand out to Lynnie offering to her something she could not see, but somehow knew she wanted. He kept his hand closed tightly around the object and handed it over to her.

Lynnie, you may open the gift that Mike has handed you. These are keys; keys that go to our new home. I bought this home for us. Lynnie, Please say you will marry me!

Lynnie was overwhelmed with joy as she threw the paper down and went over to Luke. She saw Lee take the ring out of his pocket and hand it to Luke. The ring had belonged to Grace Elizabeth's great grandmother at one time and Deb had given it to Grace Elizabeth when they were at the hospital saying goodbye when she passed away. She knew that Lynnie would want to have this ring and she offered it to Luke when he came to ask Lee and Grace Elizabeth if he could ask Lynnie to marry him.

She never knew that they had all been conspiring behind her back this whole all this time. She was so very happy that her family was all there now.

"Of course I will marry you. I love you!"

The applause came from everyone at the restaurant and Grace Elizabeth had tears rolling down her face.

"Finally Lynnie can have true happiness in her life."

Mike offered to do another toast.

"I want to thank everyone for being here this evening. I also want to welcome Luke into our family. One more thing, Sis I would like to perform your service. Annie and I both want to help you."

Annie grinned and she too had tears streaming down her cheeks. She agreed that this was a great idea. She wanted her whole family there to enjoy her happiness with her. Lee and Grace Elizabeth were both very pleased with the outcome of the evening.

"Lynnie, please do not be upset with any of us for not sharing in this evening's events with you. We have all tried very hard to surprise you with Mike and Annie moving here, Lee and I moving here, and the proposal of course. We knew that you were busy with your search…yes, I knew about that too. Lee never keeps anything from me, ever. We only want you to be happy my dear sweet girl. You deserve all the happiness in the world and I only hope that you have found it here with all of us."

"I am truly blessed to have each of you in my life. I never knew that a family could mean so much happiness. I am happy mom and I owe that happiness to you. Thank you."

Mike walked over to Lynnie and hugged her so hard he picked her up off the floor spinning her around. She hugged him back even tighter. She loved her brother and was so glad that he and Annie moved down there.

"Ok, how did you pull this one off? I know just about everyone around here and not a soul told me that you and Annie moved here. Where are you living now?"

"Off Kings Highway, over by the Y in the road near the railroad tracks."

Lynnie knew exactly where they were living now.

"Where are you and dad living now?"

"We will be living in our motorhome. We have not really decided whether we want to buy a house or not."

"How in the world did you pull off buying this restaurant without us knowing?"

"It is all in who you know and what you are willing to learn."

Lynnie liked his play on words and chuckled.

Everyone was glad that Lynnie accepted Luke's proposal and Annie knew that she wanted to do as much as she could to help her; just like she did for her and Mike in Pennsylvania when they were married in Pymatuning. Annie was pregnant and she knew she had to be careful with how much extra stress she took on too.

Luke came over and scooped Lynnie up in a big hug; giving her a very passionate, teasing kiss, he spun her around and dipped her head back like the dancers do in ballroom dancing. He was very happy and he wanted everyone in the world to know it.

The waitress came over to pour more wine.

"So when is the big day?"

"Well, we really have not thought about the date just yet."

"I think we should get married today, right now, while we are all here. What do you think Lynnie?"

Somehow, Lynnie knew this was part of the evening's game plan too. As she looked around the room, Lynnie saw a piece of paper being passed around behind the backs of those trying to get to Mike. Like a bunch of kids passing a note in grade school! Lynnie looked at Grace Elizabeth and Lee who both looked back giving her a nod of approval. Mike and Annie too gave a nod of approval.

"We don't have a license or anything, how can we possibly get married right here and right now?"

Just then, the piece of paper that was being passed around came into Mike's hands and he showed it to Lynnie. It just so happened to be a marriage license. How clever everyone was to go through all of this and how they all managed to keep it from her was a surprise to Lynnie. She had no idea that her family could be so sneaky and she was so glad they had been.

"Man are you a clever devil! It appears like you have everything under control. Sneaky, sneaky man! Yes, I will marry you here and now, but I will only marry you here and now under one condition."

"What condition is that?

"That Lee gives me away."

Lee accepted and he too had tears on his cheeks. He was surprised that she asked him to give her away. He was grateful to be asked and accepted this honor for her. Luke brushed his brow as if to say "*phew, glad everything played out like I wanted it to*" and everyone waited for Mike to get his Bible so he could read the same sermon for Lynnie that had been read at his wedding.

When he came back into the restaurant, he asked everyone to take their positions and he would begin the ceremony.

*Dearly beloved, we are gathered
here today to witness the union of Luke and
Lynnie in Holy matrimony.*

Lynnie remembered the same words
being said at Mike and Annie's wedding and
know she knew how Annie felt that day.

*It is said in Genesis 2:18-24 - The
Lord God said, "It is not good for the man to
be alone. I will make a helper suitable for
him." Now the Lord God had formed out of
the ground all the beasts of the field and all
the birds of the air. He brought them to the
man to see what he would name them, and
whatever the man called each living
creature, that was its name. So, the man
gave names to all the livestock, the birds of
the air and all the beasts of the field. But,
for Adam no suitable helper was found. So
the Lord God caused the man to fall into a
deep sleep; and while he was sleeping, he
took one of the man's ribs and closed up the
place with flesh. Then the Lord God made a
woman from the rib he had taken out of the
man, and he brought her to the man. The
man said, "This is now bone of my bones
and flesh of my flesh; she shall be called
'woman,' for she was taken out of man".
For this reason, a man will leave his father*

*and mother, be united to his wife, and they
will become one flesh.*

Lynnie's tears were freely streaming
down her face when she realized she had
never been this happy before.

*I have been reunited with my family
this year when I learned of my sister Lynnie.
I thank God that she and I have been
brought together. I thank God that Grace
Elizabeth and Lee loved each other enough
to have a child of their own. I thank God for
my beautiful wife Annie, every day, I thank
God for waking up and seeing his precious
hands at work building another beautiful
day for us to enjoy. I want to thank God for
bringing Luke and Lynnie together. They
are so in love and so fit to be united as man
and wife. They need each other like the
flowers need rain, like a child needs their
mother, like everything in life needs God.*

Lynnie repeated the words "*like a
child needs their mother*" over in her mind.
She liked that saying.

*Now, Lynnie, please repeat after me
- I, Lynnie, take you Luke, to be my wedded
husband. To have and to hold, from this day
forward, for better, for worse, for richer, for
poorer, in sickness and in health, to love and*

*to cherish, until death do us part. I hereto
pledge you my faithfulness. Luke, please
repeat after me – I, Luke, take you Lynnie, to
be my wedded wife. To have and to hold,
from this day forward, for better, for worse,
for richer, for poorer, in sickness or in
health, to love and to cherish until death do
us part. I hereto pledge you my faithfulness.*

"Can we have the rings please."

Lynnie looked at him with raised
eyebrows; she did not have a ring for Luke.
Lee handed Luke the ring that Deb had
given to Grace Elizabeth. When he went to
place the ring on her finger, she recognized
it and knew where it had come from. She
looked at Grace Elizabeth and started crying
again; tears of joy. After he slid the ring
onto her finger, she held it up for everyone
to see and proudly displayed it with love.

*I now pronounce you man and wife.
Luke, you may kiss your bride, my sister
Lynnie.*

The cheer from the restaurant could
be heard down the street and more patrons
came into the restaurant to see why
everyone was so happy and why everyone
was cheering. It just so happened that Amy
had been downtown at the time shopping at

one of the bookstores in town. She too came into the restaurant to see why everyone was cheering. Lynnie saw Amy when she came in and walked towards her. Amy saw her coming and started to walk away.

"Amy wait!"

Annie heard Lynnie holler the name Amy and turned to see what was going on. Annie met eye to eye with her. The tears strolled down Annie's cheeks when she walked over to her.

"Annie?"

"Amy?"

The two girls were amazed that they too had been reunited on such a wonderful day. Amy was not sure if being reunited at a wedding was good luck or bad luck, but she was glad that she finally had seen her sister. It had been a very, very long time since the two girls had laid eyes on each other. Annie smiled and Amy smiled back. The two girls hugged each other, crying tears of happiness.

Lynnie was sitting at the table watching the two girls, thinking to herself "another broken circle of life has been made whole again" how exciting that her special day had played out so well. She felt blessed to be part of such a loving family and now she had her own family.

Chapter Twelve

After the wedding and everyone had a chance to do some catching up, Lynnie asked Luke, "Why did you give me that list written out on a piece of paper?"

"So you can keep that piece of paper in your Bible and always remember this day and the different events that took place."

"See, this is why I love you so much. You think of "*our*" future and not just yours."

While they were sitting there enjoying each other's company, Lee received a phone call on his cell. Lynnie heard the phone ring and watched as he answered the call.

"I need to take this call, do you mind if I take it outside so I am not interrupting the party?"

"No not at all."

Lee walked outside with his cell phone to his ear. Lynnie was curious as to who could be calling Lee right now. She wondered if it was about Lisa or Rick.

A short while later, he returned inside and walked over to Grace Elizabeth and whispered something in her ear. The two disappeared into the kitchen afterward. Lynnie could not help but wonder who was calling Lee's cell phone.

"Did you see that?"

"Yeah, I wonder what is going on."

The two waited anxiously for Lee and Grace Elizabeth to return so they could find out who the call was from and if it had anything to do with them. A short while later, Lee came back into the room alone. He walked over to them and asked them to follow him into the kitchen.

"It appears that Lisa has been sent to a mental institution. They found her after she had tried to commit suicide by taking a whole bottle of prescription pills she had bought off the street. She was in the hospital for a while until she recovered enough to be sent to the mental facility."

"Which hospital is she in now?"

"She is in a hospital in northeastern Pennsylvania. They have a unit there specifically to treat patients in an infirmary type setting."

"Is she able to have visitors?"

"Yes she is and your mother and I are going up to see her. Would you be interested in going along?"

"Well, yes I would. I still would like to talk to her and get some things straightened out. Do you think she is up for that?"

"Well, I guess we really won't know until we get there and see how she is, but we can sure try. We plan on heading up there as soon as possible. I am going to see if Mike and Annie will keep an eye on the restaurant while we are away. Luke, what are your plans? Are you able to go along or do you need to be here at your store?"

"I would love to be able to support my wife, so I would like to go along."

"I guess we can leave whenever you are ready. Will we be taking the motorhome or flying."

"We will travel in the motorhome so we have everything we need with us. We all need to get our things ready that we are going to take and be ready to leave in the morning; unless that is too quick?" They all shook their heads and agreed that leaving in the morning would be just fine.

Luke immediately left to get staff in place to cover the store during his absence. Lynnie went home to pack up some things for her and Luke to take. Grace Elizabeth left the kitchen, went back out to the crowd of people to announce that they would be leaving.

"I would like everyone's attention please."

While she waited for the room to become quiet, Lee left the restaurant to get the motorhome ready for the trip north.

"I am so very glad and excited that everyone had the opportunity to join us today to celebrate the marriage of Lynnie and my new son-in-law, Luke. I am sure they too appreciate seeing each of you. It is with a saddened heart that I must close the celebration down earlier than expected. We have received some pretty important news concerning a family member, my mother, who has been admitted to the hospital up north in Pennsylvania and we need to leave in the morning to travel up there. It is of great importance that I share with you that the situation is no longer life threatening, but my mother is not out of the woods just yet. I apologize to all of you again, but we really need to be there. Thank you all for coming and please enjoy the rest of your day."

Grace Elizabeth then proceeded to leave the restaurant and head home to help Lee get ready for the trip to Pennsylvania. Mike and Annie knew they would be there to help with the restaurant and keep things in order for everyone until they returned home; when everything was stable enough for them to return.

Lynnie was a little concerned that maybe asking too many questions would not be appropriate for someone in Lisa's state of mind. She pondered not asking any at all and decided quietly to herself that she would see how things were when they arrived. She suddenly was saddened at the thought of Lisa trying to commit suicide; wondering what could be so bad in her life that she wanted to end it. After all, she was the one who was the reason for Lynnie and Grace Elizabeth being apart all those years, the death of Tammy, and Terry's demise. What could have been so bad Lynnie wondered?

Grace Elizabeth was struggling with the thought of seeing her mother after all these years apart, after all the trouble that was caused by her, and all the torment people endured due to her. She also wondered if seeing her was the right thing.

Grace Elizabeth silently asked God for strength.

"Dear Lord, please help me see the good in my mother while we are at the hospital with her. Please give me the strength to be a mature adult and not seek to cause her more pain or myself more anguish. Please comfort my daughter and the thoughts I am sure are running through her mind. Please also comfort the rest of the family who are not able to visit the hospital. Most importantly, please keep my mother safe from harm and help her heal. In Jesus name, I pray. Amen."

She knew that asking for the Lord's help was the best she could do right now and she had faith in Him to provide comfort and care to her mother.

"Lynnie, are you ok? Will you be able to confront your grandmother knowing that she is lying in the hospital healing? Lynnie, I want you to lean on me and use me for strength. Together we can conquer our fears and help each other through life. Please never forget that I am here for you and I love you with all of my heart."

Lynnie managed to crack a slight smile and hugged Luke. Lynnie thanked Luke for being so understanding and appreciated the offer of his shoulder.

"Luke I know you will be there for me. Thank you for offering me your shoulder, I am sure I will need it before everything is resolved; if it even can be. I do need to remember to say a prayer for her even though she is not my favorite person lately, but I know it is the right thing to do. Will you pray with me?"

Luke agreed.

"Dear Lord, please keep my grandmother safe from harm. I have tried to forgive her in my mind, but I am struggling with this and need your help. Please comfort my mom and Lee during this time. Lord, please give my husband Luke the courage and strength to support me through life and thank you for bringing us together. In Jesus name, Amen."

"Amen."

Luke hugged her tightly and she cried for a minute on his shoulder; tears of comfort and happiness that they were together and she was no longer alone. She had all the strength and courage she needed right there in her arms.

The next morning, bright and early, everyone was ready to pack up the motorhome and head north to Pennsylvania. Mike and Annie stopped by to offer their hand if anyone needed some help. Lee was inside helping Luke and Lynnie get their bags arranged while Grace Elizabeth was outside talking with Mike and Annie.

"Lynnie, I need you to know that your mother is very upset. She is concerned about Lisa and really not sure how she is going to handle seeing her in the hospital like this, especially a mental hospital. Please help me keep your mom's comfort in mind. I need to make sure she doesn't have any problems herself. Can you help me watch her Lynnie?"

"Absolutely! I would be upset to think that mom's comfort was not at the top of my list. She is my concern as much as she is yours Lee. We will keep a really close eye on her."

Grace Elizabeth popped her head inside long enough to see if everyone was ready to go.

"Yes, we are all ready."

Grace Elizabeth asked that everyone come out and say goodbye to Mike and Annie.

"Can we say a prayer together before you all leave?"

With everyone bowing their heads in prayer, Mike began his prayer, with a grim tone to his voice he said, "Dear lord, please watch over my family as they travel to see my grandmother in the hospital. Please give everyone the strength to endure the trip. Please give everyone the ability to focus on the task at hand. Please also keep an extra close eye on my mother Lord; give her the courage to face her fears with your presence everywhere she goes. Help Lynnie get the answers she is looking for. Give Lee the extra courage to keep everyone out of harm's way and the strength of love through You. Please give Luke the guidance and trust in You to keep Lynnie safe and comforted when she needs it. Please also give my Grandma Lisa a guiding light and shimmer of hope through your love. In Jesus name, Amen."

Once all of the goodbyes were said, the motorhome slowly traveled out of sight while Mike and Annie watched it pull away yet again.

Lee drove towards exit 86 on Interstate 26 where he resumed his westbound travel towards Interstate 95 north. Lee decided to drive until he reached the same RV resort in Roanoke Rapids, North Carolina. He knew they could have a good night's rest there and begin their travel again towards Pennsylvania.

Grace Elizabeth was contemplating more memories that she had tried so desperately to leave buried. She rested her head back on the seat, recalling more of her childhood with Lisa.

I knew that I was going to be grounded for sure if anyone found out I had had lied about going to a school vigil for a classmate who had been killed in a car accident. I also had decided that spending time with my friends was more important than going home and cleaning the house all day. So, I stayed out all night with my friends and had the time of my life. No adults, just teenagers all sharing some fun times together. While there was a lot of drinking and pot smoking all around me, I chose not to participate in any pot smoking, but did have a sip or two of a bottle that was being passed around. Once I realized I did not like the taste of it and it burned my nose when I swallowed it, I had enough and decided not to drink it anymore. When daybreak came, all of the teenagers had to go back home and I knew that I was going to be in so much trouble. When I walked through the door, Lisa was waiting for me with her hand on her hip, and tone of voice blaring, "Were you drinking? I smell pot on you, were you smoking pot? Let me smell your breath young lady! I bet you had fun being a little whore to all those boys, didn't you? Get over here so I can smell your breath!" Jerking me closer to her and gripped by my arm, I knew that I was in trouble and there was no getting out of it this time. I no sooner made it three steps in front of her; she grabbed me and threw me up against the wall. When I hit the floor, she was on top of me in the blink of an eye, slapping my face, and pulling my hair. She started screaming at me again, "How dare you smoke pot and then come into MY house! You stink from it! You had better hope I don't find any on you or you will be grounded for the rest of your life! I will call the police and have you thrown in jail!" While she was still slapping my face and pulling my hair, I rolled over to get her off me and she fell into the refrigerator smacking her head. She accused me of throwing her into it and told everyone that I was beating her up after I had been out smoking pot with my friends from school. I had so many bruises on my arms and face that I looked like I had been beaten by a gang of punks. Lisa made me go to school all beat up like that and I looked hideous.

It was not long and Lee pulled the motorhome into the RV Resort in Roanoke Rapids. Grace Elizabeth realized she had fallen asleep and woke up when the motorhome came to a stop. During the trip while she was sleeping, Lynnie and Luke had been sorting through pictures and keeping each other company. Luke had been talking with Lee about the motorhome and had considered buying one, so Lee was helping him figure out the details. No one bothered Grace Elizabeth and let her sleep knowing that she needed the rest.

The men set everything up outside and the women worked inside.

"How are you doing mom? Are you feeling ok?"

"Yes, I feel fine and there really is no need for you to keep asking me that

Lynnie. I appreciate your concern, but I am fine, really."

"Ok, but I know this is going to be a stressful visit and I want you to know that I will be keeping my eye on you and checking with you to make sure you continue to do fine."

Grace Elizabeth hugged her and thanked her again for her concern.

Dinner was potato salad and hamburgers cooked over the campfire that Luke had started. Lynnie was still wondering if this visit was going to be beneficial or if she would have to curtail her questions for another time; although, she preferred to ask her questions now since she did not anticipate seeing her Grandma Lisa after this trip. She knew she had to figure out how to achieve her goals and still be empathetic to her grandmother. Lee was tired from driving and went to grab a shower before lying down for the night. Grace Elizabeth, Luke, and Lynnie went for a walk around the resort to spend some time in the evening air and stretch their legs after riding all day. They knew it wouldn't be long before they were showered and in bed for the night too. There seemed to be a sense of silent calm in the air that everyone was feeling.

In the morning, everyone was rested and ready to begin the final part of the trip up to Pennsylvania. Luke was outside helping Lee get everything put away and learning about the motorhome. Grace Elizabeth and Lynnie were inside securing everything for the trip. It was not long and they were back on Interstate 95 heading north towards Interstate 270 and then on to Interstate 70, towards Breezewood, and back onto Interstate 80. When they reached the little town where the institution was, everything had closed up for the night. There was a Wal-Mart nearby so they decided to pull off in the back corner and sleep there. The evening was quiet, but everyone was tired so it made it easier to get some rest.

Early in the morning, they decided to check in with the hospital to see if they could visit Lisa. Grace Elizabeth called to talk with her doctor who was not available when she called. She left a message with the secretary who said the doctor would return her call when he returned from doing his morning rounds with the patients. At about nine, Grace Elizabeth's cell phone rang and it was Dr. Anderson calling her.

"Hi Dr. Anderson, this is Grace Elizabeth, my mother is one of your patients, Lisa. She is the patient that has been in your infirmary for attempted suicide."

"Yes, Grace Elizabeth, how can I help you?"

"My family and I came as soon as we heard the news and we would like to see mom if she is able to have visitors."

"I am glad that you and your family were able to make the trip up to see your mom. I would like to have a family meeting prior to you visiting with her. This is a requirement for all patients who reside here at the hospital. It is a necessary precaution due to the nature of our patients."

"Ok, we are able to meet whenever you can. How does today sound, maybe late this morning?"

"I am available this morning until around eleven, but then I will be off the grounds until tomorrow."

"Would it be ok if we came now and met with you?"

Dr. Anderson agreed. Grace Elizabeth told her family that they had to have a meeting with the hospital physician prior to being able to see Lisa and they were meeting with him this morning, as soon as everyone was ready to go. It did not take them long to get ready and make their way to meet with Dr. Anderson.

When they arrived at Dr. Anderson's office, they had to wait for him to return. He had been helping with a patient who was being put in a seclusion room to keep from hurting the other patients. When he finally made it back to his office, he apologized for not being there and asked them all to come into his office.

"I am glad that you were all able to make it today. Let me get Lisa's folder out and I will give you some information, give me just a moment to get myself together here."

Once he had everything in place, Dr. Anderson continued, "It is documented here in her chart that she attempted to commit suicide by consuming very large doses of pain pills and what appeared to be some other street drugs. We are waiting for the actual toxicology report, but the street drugs appeared to be meth-based or methamphetamine-based I should say. When they found Lisa, she was lying on the floor completely unresponsive and paramedics were called. They revived her and transported her to the hospital."

"Can you tell me who found her?"

"The name on the file is Karen. Do you know who Karen is?

"Yes, she is my sister. We have not been in contact for many years so I am sure she would have no idea any of us are even here."

"She did not answer any of my calls when I tried to reach her to ask a few questions about Lisa. I am not sure if I even have the right phone number, but I did try to contact her."

"I am sure she must just be busy and has not had a chance to return your call yet." Is there anything I can help you with?"

"Well, I do need to know about your mother's medical history so I know if she has any underlying conditions or problems that we need to watch for. I also will need next of kin information for her chart; we collect this on all of our patients here for obvious reasons. I will also need to have contact information from a family member to have on record that is not the same as the next of kin, someone who can be trusted with private medical information in case the next of kin is not available for whatever reason; like a backup contact."

"You can list me as the next of kin and my daughter Lynnie as the secondary backup. We will leave our contact information with you today while we are here."

"There is something else I need to tell you before you go see her. She keeps mumbling the name Rick. Does this name mean anything to you?

"Yes, that is Lynnie's father's name."

"Another name she keeps mumbling is Terry. Do you know who this person is?"

"Yes, that was a little boy who was killed. He was the child of Lisa and Rick."

Dr. Anderson had an odd look on his face.

"Rick is Lynnie's father?" He said pointing at Lynnie. "Lisa is your grandmother, do I have this right?"

"Yes, Rick and Lisa had a child together and the little boy's name was Terry. He was killed when he shot himself in the head with a gun while at Lisa's house."

"Ok, now that we know the meaning behind the names; why do you suppose she is asking for these people now?"

"Seems to be a good question. Did you ask her?"

"Yes, we have all tried to get her to share more about these people she keeps calling out and mumbling for. She would only tell us that we would not understand and never say any more about it."

"I am surprised she would not tell you who they were. Both Terry and Rick seem to be important people or she would not have them on her mind after such a tragic event."

"Do any of you have any questions for me?"

"Yes, I do. Is my grandmother able to hold a conversation; enough to answer questions?"

"Yes, she is fairly cognitive now and I am sure will be surprised to see you folks here today. Any other questions?"

"Is there anything we need to watch for while we are visiting her today? Will she have any problems that we need to be aware of?"

"I would ask that if she starts getting upset, abusive, verbally disruptive, or combative in any way that you alert the staff immediately. Other than that, all I can say is good luck to you folks and let any of us know if you have any further questions."

Dr. Anderson handed Grace Elizabeth and Lynnie both his card that had all of his contact information on it and asked them to sign the documents stating they were the emergency family contacts.

"There is one more thing, we will need to make preparations for Lisa's discharge and I would like to know where the family intends for her to go upon leaving the hospital."

Grace Elizabeth and Lynnie just looked at each other, but neither offered an answer for him. The room fell silent.

"Well I guess we can work on that while she is here with us and come to an acceptable conclusion. But I do want you to keep this in mind so when I ask you again later down the road; you will have an answer for me."

Grace Elizabeth agreed that she would give this some thought and would let Dr. Anderson know if she figured out where Lisa would be able to go after discharge.

The time came for them to go to the ward where Lisa was residing. Grace Elizabeth and Lee were the first to get signed in and get their visitor's pass. Lynnie and Luke had to wait for extra seats to be brought down for them before they were able to go into the room. As they were following the staff lady down the hall, a loud siren started blaring and "code orange in the women's ward, staff requiring immediate response" was repeated over the intercom system. They just looked at each other wondering if this was a safe place for them to be. The staff lady assured them this response call was in a different part of the facility and not even in the same building as they were. When they arrived at Lisa's ward, the staff lady stopped outside the door.

"Now when I open this door and let you two on the ward, we have to get inside and get the door locked back up as quickly as possible. The ladies on this ward are older, but are still fast on their feet and like to make a run for the door whenever it is opened. There is also a lady who will wait by the door if staff leave the ward so she can charge the staff when they come back, so when I say it's ok, we need to get on the ward quickly so I can get the door locked."

Grace Elizabeth and Lee agreed and were ready when she said, "now!" Once they were inside the ward and behind the locked door with the patients, Grace Elizabeth felt very uncomfortable about her surroundings. Lee could sense this and stayed close beside her while they were there.

"Before I forget, please make sure you turn off your cell phone ringer and keep your possessions with you at all times. We have to make sure our patients are not provided with contraband of any kind and do not steal your belongings while you are here visiting."

Grace Elizabeth was the first to go in and see her mother. Taking a deep breath and asking Lee to wish her luck, she opened the door and walked in. Lisa was sitting in a rocking chair looking out the window. When she turned to see who was coming in her room, her eyes met with Grace Elizabeth's eyes. She just sat there looking at her without saying a word. The tears welled up in her eyes and she could not help but let them role down her cheeks, still not saying a word.

Grace Elizabeth had a similar complexity to meeting eye to eye with Lisa. She did not say a word either, just stood there looking at her mother with a cold, blank stare, and tears welling up in her eyes.

"What are you doing here?"

"Well I see you appear to be your old ungrateful self mother. I heard you were here and came to make sure you were ok."

Lisa just sat there trying to make sense of why Grace Elizabeth of all people was there in her hospital room.

"Why you of all people? I thought you were dead or maybe it was just wishful thinking."

"Really mother, I came to see you. Your granddaughter Lynnie is here too. I will go get her so we can all sit and talk together."

"I do not see where talking with you will do anybody any good. Why not just send Lynnie in; I would love to see my granddaughter. You can go home and just leave me alone. I do not care to see you ever again Grace Elizabeth and I will not mix any words with you. I do not want you here."

"I do not care if you want me here or not. I am here and we have some things to discuss with you before we leave, so you might just as well get use to the fact that you cannot shove me out the door against my will. I will be right back with Lynnie and all three of us will sit here and have a talk, mother."

Grace Elizabeth left the room slamming the door behind her. Lisa sat inside appalled to think that she showed up there at the hospital. Lee could see the hurt in Grace Elizabeth's eyes.

"Are you ok my dear? You look like you just saw a ghost."

"Oh that bitter, evil old woman just tried to throw me out of here. I am not leaving without getting the answers I came here to get. No matter how hateful she is."

Lynnie and Luke were coming around the corner when Lynnie saw how upset her mother was.

"Mom, are you ok?"

"Yes, that bitter old woman just tried to throw me out of here and I am not going anywhere. I was just shocked at how she just told me she thought I was dead and pretty much wished that statement were true. She wants to see you Lynnie, but does not want to see me at all. I told her that none of us were leaving until we had a chance to speak our minds with her and get some questions answered."

"Good, I am ready to go head to head with this crazy old woman if that is what she wants."

"Keep in mind, you are here looking to this bitter old woman for answers, so upsetting her will do you no good at succeeding in getting your answers and that's the reason why you are here in the first place."

They agreed with him and decided to just play nice with Lisa and see how far they could get.

"If she is ok with seeing Lynnie, then Lynnie will probably have to be the one to ask her any questions. Otherwise, we may be here a lot longer than we need to be."

They were trying to put together a game plan when Grace Elizabeth spoke up.

"I have to try to find peace with this woman, even if it rips my heart out. I don't want to leave here without resolving my past with her."

"Well mom, I am going to go in there with Luke and introduce the two. Maybe she will play nice with me if we are both there together."

Grace Elizabeth and Lee agreed that no one should be in the room alone with Lisa at any time. She was too spiteful and could not be trusted not to cause harm to any of them. Lynnie and Luke agreed and opened the door to go into Lisa's room.

"Hi grandma, how are you?"

"I am fine Lynnie, how are you my dear. Who is this young man with you?"

"Grandma, this is my husband Luke. Luke meet my Grandma Lisa."

Luke extended his hand to shake Lisa's hand, and she grabbed him and hugged him rather than shaking his hand. Luke was startled by her strength and tried to keep his composure and try not to giggle.

"Pleased to meet you, Grandma Lisa."

"I am pleased to meet you too Luke."

"Well, Lynnie, what brings you here to see me?"

"Honestly, grandma, I need to talk to you about some things and more than anything I wanted to make sure that you were ok."

"Seems that is the buzz of the day, everyone wants to talk to me about one thing or another. Why now? I don't recall anyone coming to my home to talk with me or visiting me anywhere for that matter to talk to me. Why now, I ask?"

"Let's face it grandma, you are not the most pleasant person to be around and people feel threatened to be near you sometimes. I have some questions that I need to ask you and I want you to be honest with me too."

"I will be as honest as I can be, but I am not guaranteeing anything, not even that I will answer any of your questions. So let's not get your hopes up too high deary. I would suggest that if you want to ask me anything you better ask now while I am ready to answer you."

"Ok, can we all sit down. I would feel more comfortable sitting down talking with you rather than standing."

"Sure, let me get some chairs for you two and we will sit here and talk for a bit."

Lisa walked over to the wall and pushed the button on the wall so she could ring the front desk. A moment later, a lady's voice came over Lisa's intercom.

"Yes, Lisa, how can I help you?"

"Can you bring four chairs down to my room for my guests please?"

"Sure, give me just a moment to gather them up for you and I will be right there."

Lisa thanked the lady and Lynnie and Luke walked out into the hall while they were waiting for the staff to get there with the chairs.

"Mom, I think she wants all of us to come in. She asked the staff to bring four chairs to her room so we could sit down."

"I am glad she is willing to talk with us. Sure would be a pain to have to come back here later."

Lynnie giggled at Grace Elizabeth's snide, but comical, remark. A moment later, the lady showed up at Lisa's room with four chairs in tow.

"Here are the chairs you asked for Lisa. Let me know if you need anything else."

Lisa thanked the lady for bringing her the chairs and invited her four visitors all into her room at the same time and offered each of them a chair to sit in.

Once everyone was sitting, Lisa said, "I understand you all seem to have questions for me. I am willing to listen to your questions, but depending on how I feel I may not be so willing to give you an answer."

"Ok, I will start. Can you tell me what kind of relationship you had with my father, Rick?"

"Well, Lynnie, you need to be more specific than that."

"Listen, I know about you and my dad. I also know about Terry. You are not hiding anything from me Grandma Lisa. I also want you to know that I have done my homework and know why you are the way you are to people. You may have been raised in a very loving family and never wanted for a thing, but you have never been truly loved. You had the love of your mom and dad, but never the love of anyone else. No one ever "wanted" you. No one ever showed you the love you were desiring. The love you had from your parents never came close to the love you demanded from others. You were looking for love, even if it was the wrong type of love. You were so greedy in your search for love, you shoved those who truly did love you out of the way, and relied on those you could love overnight at best. You wanted them to feel what you were feeling, so it never lasted long."

Lisa started to say something and Grace Elizabeth asked her to sit back down and listen to what Lynnie was saying. With a shocked look but not able to argue the point, Lisa reluctantly sat back down.

"No! Let me finish Grandma. You are a very cruel woman and it is no wonder anybody has anything to say to you, nice or otherwise. You have treated my mother like garbage and you were the reason that I was taken away from her when I was little. Why would you do that? How could you do that? That is the only question I have for you, why, just why?"

Lisa looked at her granddaughter with pain in her eyes. She knew that Lynnie was right but she was compelled to be defensive. Lisa wanted to protect her identity as being a cruel woman and she really was not that way at all. It was her "*front*" that people saw and Lynnie had seen through it.

"Before you answer that question, I am here to get the same question answered. Why mom? Why would you be so outright mean and cruel? What did I ever do to you to cause you to hate me as much as you do? Why did you take Lynnie from me and cause so much hurt in this family? Why, I ask you, why?"

Lisa knew she was going to have to show her vulnerable side with them both coming at her with the same question. They were looking for the same answers.

"I guess now is the time to share this with you, *both* of you. You are right Lynnie; I have never had the true love of anyone other than my parents. I have always been quick to bring men into my life and get hurt, but never have had the true love of anything more than my mom and dad. Grace Elizabeth, when I was pregnant with you I was very much in love with your father Mel. He was the most amazing person in the world and I truly loved him. I did not want to share that love with you or anyone else. I wanted it all to myself. I convinced myself that if I hated you and treated you badly it would cause your father to pay more attention to me for that reason. Maybe he would feel sorry for me. I don't know. It may not have been the right thing to do, but I did it. I had his attention and everyone else just fell in line with my attitude. I grew mean and hateful knowing that if I had a wall up that no one could get through then I could never get hurt again.

Being so hateful towards people was my way of getting the attention that I craved. I was not able to get the attention any other way, so I figured I would get it no matter what I had to do."

"So, why did you sleep with my father and have a child with him? What brought you to do that Grandma?"

"I felt close to Rick and knew that if I slept with him then I would have control over his feelings too, even if only for a short time. Not realizing that I would get pregnant so quickly, I continued to have sex with him for quite a while. All the time, knowing that I had no feelings for him whatsoever, but knew that I could control him that way. I used him to get what I wanted."

"I appreciate your honesty mother, but I do not understand how you could feel so lonely knowing that your family loved you."

"I know that my family loved me, but it was not the love I was craving. I wanted the love of a man, of someone other than my parents, anyone, the deep 'grit your teeth' kind of love that you only see in the movies. I wanted to know that I was going to be safe and cherished for the rest of my life, as long as I had that kind of love … especially of a man who was willing to take care of me and love me for the person I am, or was at the time. I was jealous of you Grace Elizabeth. I was jealous over the fact that everybody loved you and trusted you. I wanted that for myself. I wanted what you had, so I took what you had away. I was drunk on the control I had over you and your life."

"And all this time I beat myself up trying to find out what I did to make you hate me so much. There was nothing I could do to protect myself or my life from you, nothing! You were determined to see me fail and I had no control over what you were doing."

"Of course you had no control, I planned it that way. Taking you down was not the easiest thing I have ever done Grace Elizabeth. You were everything I wanted to be and I had to crumble that, no matter what it took for me to bring you down, I was determined, very determined to make you hate me. I built my life around making you as miserable as I could. The more miserable you were, the more control I knew I had over you."

"I just don't understand why you could do that to my mother, Grandma Lisa. You caused so much pain for my mother and for me too. I have spent my life trying to figure out how you could pull off such an arrogant life for yourself and then it dawned on me that you had never had the love you were craving. You had everything else, so it had to be that. I struggled with this for a lot of years and took counseling to help bring what was inside me out to share with others. I owe that much to you. You helped me realize that not everyone was as evil or cruel as you. Why didn't you just own up to this with my mom? There was no reason to carry it on for as long as you have. Too many people have been hurt by you and will always have hateful feelings toward you. Don't you ever want to heal that hurt grandma?"

"Oh Lynnie, you just don't quite understand me well enough yet to know that I just don't care. I could care less what other people think of me or what I do. I have built up my barrier wall so high that even I cannot see over the top of it. I am too old to change anything now. I don't even want to change anything. I am fine the way I am."

"I may be new to this family as far you are all concerned, but I have sat back and watched my wife, your daughter, hurt for far too long. Lisa, I disagree with you saying that you are too old and that you don't want to change. If that were the case, then why are we all sitting here listening to you spill your heart to us now? It is obvious to me that you want to change and you are asking for help in your own little way. You want us to offer to help you so you can deny it and drag it on for as long as you see fit. Well, the time has come for this wall to be brought down. No more lies, no more hate, no more being cruel, no more hiding behind the person you thought you wanted to be. From this day forward, we are all going to work together to bring the real you out and show you how much people do care for you and how much you really do care for others. Is everybody in agreement here?"

"I am all for helping my mother become the person I know she can be."

"I want to help too."

"I am here to help as well."

"Lisa, this is not going to be easy for you and we all know that, but we are all here to help you. Are you willing to let us help you Lisa?"

"After all I have put you through in your life Grace Elizabeth, you are still willing to help me? Lynnie, you too? I don't understand. I treated you both so badly for so long and you are here to help me? I cannot wrap my head around this; really I am not sure I even want to."

"Listen mother we want to help you. I for one know that you can be a good person. I knew that you were not as mean and hateful as you portrayed yourself to be. I knew your interior was as broken as your exterior, but never knew how to glue you back together. Mom, listen to me. I am here to help you. We can start with a clean slate and work on our future together. There is no reason to relive the past other than to strengthen our future. Our lives have not been as good as we would want for each other, but there is no reason to hide anymore, none whatsoever. We are all adults now. What happened in the past cannot be changed, so let's move on and work on building a future together. I am willing to work on this are you?"

"Yes, I guess I am, but how are we going to undo all of the hurt from the past?

I did a lot of damage to you Grace Elizabeth and to you too Lynnie. How are either of you going to be able to move past that and help me be a better person?"

"Grandma we seriously do love you, even though you caused so much hate and discontent for us. We have seen the other side of you and know that you can be a good person. When we figured out the reason behind your meanness, we knew that we could help heal you and move on from this. That is what a real family does and that is what love is all about. Unconditional love means looking beyond the hurt. I want to help you and I want you to let me help you."

"If the two of you think you can fix everything I have broken, I am willing to let you try."

"We are not talking about fixing whatever you broke mom, we are talking about fixing *you* so you can heal from the inside out. The things you broke cannot be fixed, but *you* can be and that is what we need to do; fix you. Then you can work on fixing the things you broke, that will show you the love you have been craving."

Lee looked at Lynnie with a smile on his face.

"Now this is the true meaning of a complete circle. We started out with you Lisa being the nicest woman in the world, to turning into this vicious person that no one wanted to be around, and now the same people that you tried to destroy are here to help you be the person you are capable of being. The broken circle of life has been made whole again with the love of this family. It simply goes to show that if you take the time to figure out why someone is hurting so badly and causing pain towards others, including themselves, that the pain is deep within. This type of pain needs to be healed from the inside out. It may take some time and a lot of work, but this can be accomplished when everyone is willing to work together. Work on building the *full* circle, not just part of it, and it makes the circle stronger."

Grace Elizabeth appreciated that the Broken Circle of Life had been made whole and was determined to keep it from falling apart again.

So started their journey of forgiving and helping heal the family. Let it be known that there is nothing stringer than the power of forgiveness. It can heal and protect you from the deepest darkest moments of your life. Learn to forgive others, heal yourself from the inside out.

Mark 11:25 (KJV) - And when ye stand praying, forgive, if ye have ought against any: that your Father also which is in heaven may forgive you your trespasses.

CHARACTER LIST

Amy - Annie's twin sister

Annie - Mike's wife

Connie - Rick sister

Deb - Lynnie's stepmother

Dr. Anderson - Lisa's physician

Grace Elizabeth - Mother to Mike and Lynnie

Grandma Lisa - Mother to Grace Elizabeth

Karen - Grace Elizabeth's sister

Lee - Father to Mike, Husband to Grace Elizabeth

Luke - Lynnie's husband

Lynnie - child of Grace Elizabeth and Rick

Nancy - Babysitter

Rick - Father to Lynnie and Terry

Ron - Rick's cousin

Tammy - Childhood friend of Lynnie

Terry - Brother to Lynnie, child of Lisa and Rick

Tim - Lynnie's first husband

ABOUT THE AUTHOR

"I started writing poems when I was just a little girl. I never did much with anything I wrote other than read it a few times and then put it away. Over the years, everything I had written was lost or destroyed, but the memories I had still lingered on in my mind. We all struggle with things deep within us and outside of us that intrigues our senses enough to want to tell the world about it; why not share what stimulates us and sparks our emotions through a book."

Visit www.tlbliss.com for more information and links to purchase other stories written by TL Bliss.